# A HOME FOR HIS OMEGA

## HOBSON HILLS OMEGAS: BOOK ELEVEN

## C.W. GRAY

# CONTENTS

HENRY

"You're a good girl, Sophie, and we're almost done," Henry Powell said softly. "Almost. Done." He put the last flourish of bright purple nail polish on the sweet brahma chicken's tiny nails. She only had one leg, but she was thriving and liked to look her best. "Remember when you first got here and didn't like to be held? Those daily bandage changes were no fun, huh?"

His friend, Sam, eyed them from outside the pen. "I remember those bandage changes. I still have the scars to prove it."

Henry snorted. "Scars? She barely pecked you."

"They're inner scars from the trauma."

"You're ridiculous." Henry blew on Sophie's nails. "She's an angel."

The one-legged chicken really was very sweet. To Henry. He did worry that she was lonely, though. She had her own small pen away from the other chickens on the animal sanctuary because they tended to pick on her. While he visited her every day, she spent most of her time alone.

"Journey and I love you, Sophie." Henry stroked gently

down her back. His dog, Journey, watched them from the safety of his pooch pouch. The Pomeranian mix smiled happily, tongue hanging out of his mouth.

"We still have goats to feed," Sam reminded him softly.

Henry flushed and set Sophie down on the shavings lining the floor. "Sorry. I didn't mean to take so long."

"It's no problem." Sam held the gate open for him. "You're good for her. I wish the other chickens weren't so mean to her."

"Teague said it was their nature to pick on the weakest, especially if it's an unfamiliar hen." Henry hated the truth in his stepbrother's words. There was nothing wrong with Sophie. She was beautiful and deserved to be accepted and loved. *Everyone does*, he reminded himself, taking a few deep breaths to ease the tightness gathering in his chest. There was a distinct possibility that Henry was getting too worked up about chicken bullies, but he couldn't help himself. He empathized with Sophie a bit too much.

The rest of the morning passed quickly. Henry and Sam fed the goats and donkeys, then let them out into the pasture behind the barn while Teague, Henry's stepbrother, took care of the chickens, pigs, and various other farm animals. Henry appreciated it because the llama they had taken in months ago was still grumpy and mean. Then there were the emus. The evil, evil emus.

Teague's animal sanctuary had been open for over a year now, and they were absolutely filled to the brim with unwanted farm animals and pets. They even had a few injured wild animals that Teague was licensed to care for.

"Ready for lunch?" Teague asked, jogging toward them from the smaller barn. The alpha pulled Sam into his arms and nuzzled his husband's neck. "I missed you."

Henry spun on his heel and walked quickly toward the house. He hated the niggling bit of envy that wormed its way into his heart. Teague and Sam had something special. Something that, in Henry's experience, wasn't common. Thinking about what he couldn't have was never pleasant. He'd much rather think about his nephew, Casey.

*There, that made me smile.*

Inside, Aunt Mia sat next to the kitchen window in her padded rocking chair, Casey snuggled in her arms and her blind Maltese, Merle, curled at her feet. Her two black cats, Luna and Dove, sat on the windowsill, enjoying the sunshine.

A herd of dogs and two pigs peeked over and through the gate blocking the kitchen from the living room. They'd only recently been banned from the kitchen during meals. It was mostly Orville and Wilbur's fault. The two pigs were experts at begging but needed to stay on their individual diets to remain healthy.

Some might complain at the overabundance of animals in their home, but Henry loved Teague and Sam's pets. He had never been allowed any when he was a child, so he enjoyed the chance to get to know all the unique personalities his stepbrother took in.

"I made you boys lunch." Aunt Mia's smile was warm, eyes kind. "Vegetable soup for you, Henry."

"My favorite." He leaned down to hug the older woman. "Thank you."

"I figured you would need a treat to deal with whoever keeps calling you."

He glared at his phone perched on the counter. Leaving it inside while he worked was the best self-care he'd ever experienced. Alas, it couldn't last.

Several missed calls and texts flashed across the screen. "Audrey has plans for the interior of my house."

"She has good taste." Mia waved a hand toward the kitchen cabinets. "I love the kitchen we did together."

He wrinkled his nose, thinking of how the kitchen looked

before the renovation. "You would have loved anything without shag carpet."

Mia chuckled. "True."

It wasn't that Audrey wasn't good at design, but rather that she was one of the pushiest people Henry knew. The house he had bought was the first thing that was *really* Henry's. It wasn't his childhood home in Connecticut or his loft apartment in Soho, both designed to impress the wealthy elite that circled the Powell family. It was an old Victorian style farmhouse in Hobson Hills, Maine, a few miles down the road from Teague and Sam.

His sister had been pushing him to begin renovations for weeks now, and he was running out of excuses to avoid it. He couldn't live with Teague and Sam forever.

Henry reluctantly grabbed his phone and went back outside. It was cold, the ground covered in wet snow and mud. Aunt Mia had told him that Maine had more than four seasons. In addition to summer, fall, winter, and spring, they also had *mud* season. The mess of the yard and pastures of the sanctuary certainly proved her point.

He fiddled with his hair for a moment, making sure he was presentable. He was rocking the wind-blown look, hair tousled and cheeks pink. Audrey wouldn't mind, but his papa would be appalled if he could see him.

"It's alright to not be perfect," he reminded himself.

Journey woofed softly, climbing up to lick his chin. That was another thing his papa would be appalled to see. Henry petted the little dog for a while. Coming to Teague's sanctuary and meeting all the animals was the best thing to ever happen to him. Journey, Sophie, and the others didn't critique or analysis him. They just loved him.

Audrey answered his FaceTime call almost immediately. "Little brother, guess where Rosalie and I are? Here's a hint. Brunch on Madison Avenue."

Rosalie Riverty's voice carried over the general cacophony of voices in the background. "It's your fav, Henny."

"Sant Ambroeus," he answered promptly, nibbling at his lip. He hadn't seen Rosalie or any of his friends from New York in over a year. Ros was one of the few he actually missed.

"Correct," Audrey cheered. "I'm having caprese invernale. What about you?"

"Vegetable soup," Henry answered. "Aunt Mia made it."

"I'm not going to lie. I'm a bit jealous."

"I know, right?" Henry sat on an old bench next to the door, shivering in the cold wind. "Don't get me wrong. Sant Ambroeus's risotto di mare is phenomenal, and I love it, but Aunt Mia's food is just better."

"True." Audrey smiled sweetly. "I emailed your contractor some plans, but what did you think of the links I sent? I want to go with an Art Deco style, maybe black and white marble in a diamond pattern. Of course, you'll need to add on to that house, since it's tiny. Are you sure you don't want to just tear it down and start over?"

Henry made a face. "Absolutely not. Also, I'm not sure Art Deco is me."

"Art Deco is everyone," Audrey said, rolling her eyes. "Trust me. I'm an expert on this."

"When will the party be?" Rosalie asked from the background.

"What party?" Audrey frowned toward their friend.

"To show off Henry's house." Rosalie laughed. "New place, new party. Right?"

Henry shuddered, bile rising in his throat.

Audrey gave him a sharp look. "Henry? What's wrong?"

He pasted a smile to his face. "Nothing at all. I should really go now. I'm meeting the contractor after lunch."

"Alright." She frowned. "Let me know how it goes, baby bumblebee."

It was Henry's turn to roll his eyes. "I'm twenty-six now, Audrey. You can't call me that anymore."

She shook her head. "You'll always be my baby bumblebee. Talk to you tonight." She blew him a kiss, then ended the call.

Journey whined from his warm, comfy spot in the pooch pouch.

Henry stroked the dog's small ears. "Don't worry. *Those* people will never come to Hobson Hills. They have no reason to."

"Henry?" Aunt Mia stood in the doorway. "Your soup is getting cold, dear."

He forced another smile. "Okay. I'm coming in now."

Lunch with Teague, Sam, and Aunt Mia was as warm and fun as usual. He sat at the table in front of the kitchen window and breathed in the savory scent of vegetable soup and fresh bread.

"What are our plans today?" Sam asked, looking around the table. "I'm cleaning house, hanging with the goats, then covering the evening shift at the pub."

"Napping for the both of us," Aunt Mia answered, patting Casey's back. "As long as we want. Then, we'll watch our soaps."

"I was going to take Casey with me to visit the goats," Sam said, a slight whine in his voice.

Aunt Mia shook her head. "Nope. He wants to stay warm and dry and watch *The Bold and the Beautiful* with me and the pets."

"Alright," Sam sighed pitifully. "I'll play with the goats all by myself."

"You'll live, honey," Teague added, leaning over to kiss Sam's cheek. "I'm scheduled at Doc Grover's for a couple of hours and have to do a minor surgery on a schnauzer. I'll come play with you as soon as I get finish."

"Promise?"

Teague chuckled and whispered something in Sam's ear, making him flush.

Henry mock gagged. "Remember the rules. No PDA at the table."

Sam laughed. "Casey doesn't complain."

"Give him time." Aunt Mia rocked the baby. "He's too young to know any better right now."

They all looked at Henry and it took him a moment to realize they were waiting for his answer to Sam's previous question. It still shook him that he was part of this family now.

"Oh, yeah. I'm going to my house for a couple of hours to do some planning."

Sam frowned. "All by yourself?"

Henry's gaze dropped to his soup, his chest tightening with familiar anxiety. One would think he could handle a little doubt or mockery since he'd dealt with it his whole life. He'd lost count of the dismissive comments and jokes sent his way through the years – *You messed up again? Do I need to use smaller words, Henny? Can't you do anything right? Just let me do it.* They all started to blend after a while.

Coming from Sam, though, it hurt far more than it should have. His friend was one of the few that really listened to Henry and tried to help instead of criticize when there was a problem.

*I can decide on a floorplan without help,* he told himself, taking a deep breath. *I'm not stupid.*

"I don't like it," Sam continued, stabbing a roll with his fork. "None of us should go anywhere alone until we know it's safe."

It took a few moments for Henry to process Sam's meaning. "Oh, you mean because of the dead guy in the woods."

"What else would I mean?" Sam shuddered.

In the fall, a body had been discovered in the woods behind Farm Fresh, a quaint store owned by the Wilson family. The man, Eugene Scott, had been murdered by someone after murdering his own wife. The whole thing had shaken the small town. The malicious violence wasn't usual in Hobson Hills.

"That was months ago," Henry said with a shrug, suddenly feeling light. Of course, Sam wouldn't mock him like that. "It was just one murder. It's not like there's a serial killer running around Hobson Hills."

"Murder isn't common here," Sam reminded him, looking worried. "Not like New York. Please don't go off by yourself, Henry. Not until the sheriff finds out who killed that guy."

"Well, I won't be alone for long. I'm meeting someone named Tomás at the house to talk through some last minute things, and then, I'm coming right back. I plan to clean out the chicken coops and put some herbs in their nesting boxes. I read online that certain herbs help with egg production and help prevent parasites." He also planned on painting Sophie's name on her coop, but he didn't think they really needed to know that.

Sam looked relieved. "Tomás is a nice guy. Definitely not a murderer."

"Are you sure about starting the renovation now?" Teague gave Henry a soft look. "Everyone keeps saying there'll probably be a few more storms to make mud season even worse."

"Carter, the guy in charge, says his crew can start on the inside." Henry smiled as he thought about his new home. "It'll take a few months to get everything done inside. Then, they can start on the outside."

"That house is older than me," Aunt Mia said with a snort. "You'd do better to tear it all down and start fresh."

"It has it charms." Henry licked his lips and grabbed another piece of bread. "The plumbing may be shit, but it has beautiful crown molding, a gorgeous fireplace, and a sweet little hand-carved reading nook in the master bedroom."

Aunt Mia sighed and patted Casey's back. "I must admit, it was beautiful back when I was a little girl. Of course, that's when people still lived there and maintained it."

"It'll be beautiful again." Henry said, excited. "This week, Carter and his team are tearing out walls and working on the plumbing and electrical issues. After that, once they install central heat and air, I can move in."

"You're welcome to stay here as long as you like," Sam took a bite of his soup.

"Seriously," Teague agreed. "Living in a work zone can be a pain. Here, you have a room of your own. Well, you and a few dogs and a cat have a room together."

Henry smiled shyly, warmth filling him. When his alpha dad had married Teague's dad, Timothy, Henry had been furious, certain that Timothy was only in it for the Powell wealth. Soon after the wedding, when his dad had changed his will to include Teague, Henry had shown up on Teague's doorstep, angry and upset, certain Teague and Timothy were both gold diggers.

He knew better now, and while he wished he had come to Hobson Hills for a better reason to begin with, he was glad he was there now.

"In any case," Teague added, "I'll be home in time to do the evening feeding, so take all the time you need."

"Good, because I'm not going near the emu." Henry snuck Journey a small bite of bread. "I only admire those assholes from a distance."

# TOMÁS

Tomás Wilson ate the last of his sandwich and struggled to ignore the sight of his friend, Juan, stuffing a whole donut in his mouth. That really couldn't be healthy, and Tomás wasn't sure he remembered how to do the Heimlich.

"Make sure to get a key from Henry when you go by the farmhouse," Carter reminded Tomás, grabbing the check from the table. "Then, meet me at the Tolliver house. I'll need your help putting in their new bathtub."

"Mmhhgh neggmhgh hepthhgh," Juan said, mouth full.

"He says he needs my help framing the bedroom addition on Peach street," Tomás translated.

Carter made a face. "Nope. I need you more. Plumbing is harder than carpentry. Juan will have to deal."

Juan swallowed his food. "Well, I am pretty amazing, so I guess I'll be alright."

Carter rolled his eyes. "Just finish the job by next week. The farmhouse is going to need all our attention, even your pitiful carpentry skills."

Juan leaned back with a grin. "No need to be jealous, man.

You're good at all kinds of things, like plunging toilets and tightening faucets."

Tomás snorted a laugh. Juan and Carter constantly teased one another about the quality of their work. In the jobs they took, Carter usually handled the plumbing, Tomás the electrical work, and Juan the building. How it had become a competition, Tomás would never know. They all pitched in when needed, so it made zero sense to him.

"Ain't no one smarter than a carpenter," Juan sang. "Ain't nothing dumber than a plumber. Everyone bitchin' about the electrician." He paused his song. "I can keep going if you want."

"Why are we friends again?" Carter asked, sighing.

"Hey there, Carter," Ted Langley sat in the booth beside them with his wife. "Heard you had a big job coming up. Who's the new client?"

Carter smiled at the older man. "Henry Powell. He bought the old Victorian farmhouse next door to the animal sanctuary."

Ted winced. "The rich fella? I already feel bad for you. Bet he'll complain about everything."

"He's a snot for sure," Elsie, Ted's wife, said, leaning over the short wall separating their booths. "Any time I see him in town, he's rushing off in his fancy car, never stopping to chat or lend a hand like others do."

"Maybe he was in a hurry," Juan said, shrugging.

Elsie snorted. "No way. I hear he's a laze-about that lives off his daddy's money. With all that wealth, you'd think he'd make time for us little folks, but no. Lynn down at the salon said he refused to let her cut that fancy hair of his. He doesn't do any shopping in town either. Thinks he's *gracing* Hobson Hills with his high and mighty presence."

Tomás arched a brow. He wouldn't let Lynn cut his hair

either. She usually only did perms for the elderly ladies of town.

"Henry seems like a nice guy," Carter said, smiling cooly. "Gramps really likes him too. I think we should all just get to know him."

"Agreed," Juan said, face unusually stern. "Making assumptions about a person usually just makes life more complicated for everyone."

Elsie sniffed, looking insulted. "Well, you boys are the ones that have to work for him. Good luck."

Tomás silently followed them from The Cozy Kitchen. *Henry Powell*, he thought to himself. He'd seen him from a distance a few times, but they'd never managed to meet. The omega rarely came to town and never spoke to any of the townspeople who visited the animal sanctuary.

Rumors like Elsie's swirled in town, claiming he was rich and stuck up, thought he was too good for the small town of Hobson Hills, etc. They even worried he'd cause problems for Sam and his aunt, Mia. How, Tomás didn't know, but the gossipmongers were sure he was no good.

Tomás tended to ignore the gossip. He had learned a long time ago that appearances were deceptive. He never formed opinions on a person without getting to know them first. Plus, as Carter had pointed out, Henry had made one friend in Hobson Hills – Gramps Wilson. That told Tomás the omega couldn't be that bad.

"Drive carefully." Carter slapped Tomás's shoulder. "See you in a few."

"A'int no one smarter than a carpenter," Juan sang softly, as he climbed into his truck.

"Oh, fuck off." Carter stomped to his own vehicle and left.

A short time later, wet snow and mud squelched beneath the tires of Tomás's heavy work truck as he pulled into the driveway of the old Victorian farmhouse. It had seen better days, but the roof was solid. At least, that's what Carter had said. It was large, two stories with a rough tower and wrap-around porch. Care had gone into building her, and he thought she must have been lovely in her heyday.

Now, though, she could really use some work. The wood siding was missing in places and what was there was rotting with age and grime. The porch sagged in the middle, the once beautiful spindles were broken and the stick detailing on the gable was in pieces. The large windows would need replacing and the door resealed as well.

He winced, thinking of how much work it would take to make her beautiful again. He was almost afraid to see the inside. *At least I'll have plenty of work for the next six months*, he thought.

Cold rain pelted his windshield, so he grabbed his thermos of coffee before he hopped out of the car. A young man stood on the porch, shivering. He looked out of place in his expensive green coat and designer jeans. Even the pricey gray dog carrier bag on his shoulder stood out.

"Tomás Wilson," he said, introducing himself and holding his hand out as he came up the steps.

"Henry," the omega said, flushing as he smiled shyly. "Gramps told me all about you and the other Wilsons. I feel like I know you already."

Tomás laughed happily. "That sounds like the old man. He'd talk for hours about his family if someone would listen."

A small, furry head poked out of the pet carrier bag. The Pomeranian mix watched Tomás with a serious expression on its little face.

"This is Journey," Henry said, smiling softly. "He's my sweet baby boy."

"Hello, Journey." Tomás held his hand out for Journey to sniff. "I have a pup of my own. Mitzy is a Havanese-mix."

Henry's shyness seemed to melt right in front of him. The omega's smile brightened, his eyes filling with joy.

"Aren't dogs the best? Journey is super smart. He sits, shakes, and speaks on command. I'm still trying to teach him to rollover, but he'll get it soon."

"Mitzy isn't the brightest, but she is fun." Tomás chuckled. "My horse, Paulo, is smart, though. Did you know horses can learn to shake hands too?"

"I didn't know that." Henry looked impressed. "We don't have any horses at the sanctuary, but we have a couple of donkeys. I wonder if I can teach them to shake."

"What other kinds of animals does the sanctuary have?" Tomás asked, suddenly enjoying the rain pattering against the roof of the old porch. At the moment, Henry and he were the only two people in the world.

Henry happily listed the animals at the sanctuary and told Tomás a few funny stories, his face glowing with happiness the whole time. "We have a chicken named Sophie who is the sweetest little thing. The other chickens pick on her, so she's all by herself. I wish…" Henry trailed off with a wistful look.

Tomás was fully invested now. He absolutely *had* to know what the omega wished for. "Here, let's sit down and you can tell me what you wish for."

Henry let Tomás lead him to the old bench next to the front door. "Well, it's silly really, and I don't know how Teague would feel about it."

Tomás opened his thermos and filled the thermos lid with coffee before handing it over to Henry. He gave the omega an encouraging look, giving him time to find his words.

Henry sipped the coffee, humming in appreciation. "Thanks for that. So, um, I want to build a chicken coop here for Sophie."

Tomás grinned. "Why would that be a bad idea? Carter said there were a few ramshackle sheds on the property. I could use one of them as a starter for the coop. It wouldn't take long at all."

"It's mud season right now," Henry pointed out, shaking his head. "It would be too hard."

"Not at all," Tomás said, waving away the omega's worry. "Don't worry about that. I'll have a coop for Sophie ready by the time you move in. Okay?"

"Really?" Henry looked excited. "It wouldn't be too hard?"

"Trust me," Tomás said, nudging Henry's shoulder with his own. "I can handle it."

"Thank you so much." Henry wiggled in place, then pulled Journey out of the dog carrier bag. "Let me show you inside the house. It may look rough at the moment, but you have to picture it all fixed up. Okay?"

"Okay." Tomás trailed after the omega as he spoke about all his plans for the house. Like most older homes, the house was full of small, cramped rooms, so opening it up would be a good start. The wiring was a mess, and the plumbing needed to be completely redone, but there were treasures to be found. At one time, someone had put a lot of love into the house.

"What kind of flooring are you thinking about?"

"Um, I don't know for sure." Henry watched Journey sniff around edges of the wall. "My sister thinks we should do some kind of Art Deco thing."

Tomás hummed to himself and bent to study the carpet in the tiny living room. It was in horrible shape and would have to be pulled up. He took a pocketknife from his back pocket and cut a square of the carpet away.

"Look at that," he said, moaning as he pulled more of the carpet away. "That's antique heart pine. Back in the day, long leaf pine trees almost went extinct from logging because everyone wanted this right here. It's making a return now, slowly but surely, but it would be a shame to cover this beauty up."

"What do you suggest?" Henry knelt beside him, close enough Tomás could smell his rich, omega scent.

The man was handsome, there was no doubt about that, but there was more pulling Tomás toward him. *His shoes*, Tomás thought, studying Henry's expensive brown boots. Everything about him shouted wealth, but those shoes had some miles on them. They were scuffed and well-worn. They stood out just like that bright smile on the omega's face when he talked about this house or the animals at the sanctuary.

After a moment, Henry elbowed him. "Tomás? What would you suggest I do with the flooring?"

Tomás shook himself. "Yeah, okay. I would pull up the carpet and take a good look at the floor. Then, we could sand it down to clean away any grime. After that, a coat of clear poly would show off all its perfect imperfections."

Henry watched him with rounded eyes, seemingly hanging on Tomás's every word. "Perfect imperfections?"

"My brother, Harper, is a woodworker, and he told me that every piece of wood has its own story to tell. Of course, there's a piece's species, grain pattern, and appearance, but if you do it right, you can show off its personality. Look at this plank here. It's warm, inviting, and you can even see a knot in the wood grain. At one time, when this plank was part of a tree, a branch grew here. Now, it's part of your home."

"We can't cover this wood up." Henry gave him a fierce look. "Everyone needs to see its story."

"Well said."

Henry's answering smile lit something in Tomás, and he fought the urge to lean over and kiss the omega. He desperately wanted to keep Henry smiling. *This job will be the death of me*, he thought, sighing.

"Sam, where are you?" Henry yelled as he ran into the goat barn. The barn was separated into three different sections and Sam was in the stall for the smaller goats.

"What?" Sam stumbled over a goat as he hurried to the stall gate. "Shit, sorry Goaty McGoatface."

Henry leaned over the stall walls, hanging down to pet one of his favorites, a brown pygmy goat named Popcorn. "Something happened."

The blood drained from Sam's face. "Is it Teague? Corey? Aunt Mia? Did the murderer get them?"

Henry rolled his eyes. "For fuck's sake, Sam. No one is dead. There's not a crazed murderer running around Hobson Hills."

Sam fell against the stall gate. "Don't scare me like that. What's happened?"

"Tomás Wilson." Henry focused on scratching under Popcorn's chin, suddenly feeling like a fool for rushing all the way home just to talk to Sam. The man was just so easy to talk to, and he always made time to listen to Henry.

Sam leaned back and studied him for a moment. "You look good when you smile like that."

Henry rolled his eyes and pulled Popcorn's ear. "I smile all the time."

"Not like this." Sam shook his head and propped his arms on top of the gate, ignoring the goats gathering behind him, slowly moving closer. "This is a *real* smile, full of joy and shit like that."

"You have such a way with words."

"Don't pull out your snooty voice," Sam said. Goaty McGoatface was the first to start nibbling on Sam's coat, but the other goats quickly followed suit. "Damn it!"

Henry snickered as the goats pulled Sam to them, the shorter ones hanging from where they'd clamped onto his clothes. "Gramps talked about his family, but there's so there's so many of them that I can't keep them all straight. Do you know anything about Tomás? Is he single?"

Sam hopped in place, trying to dislodge the goats. "Can I get some help?"

"Nope."

"You're so mean." Sam spun around in a circle, the herd of goats turning with him. "I had already moved away when the Wilsons adopted him and his sister, but Aunt Mia kept me caught up on the gossip. First, everyone talked about how he was too old for Bennett and Marco to adopt since he was eighteen. Then when he enrolled in high school with their kids, some parents were worried because he was a big guy, and no one knew anything about his past. He was only there for a semester before he graduated, so talk quieted down quickly. Other than that, I think someone told Aunt Mia he'd been in trouble with the law before. I don't know. Small town gossip isn't exactly reliable."

"I don't want to hear gossip." Henry shook his head. "What do *you* think about him?"

"He's quiet and kind," Sam said, coming to a stop and smiling at Henry. "Tomás and the other Wilsons have helped us several times here at the sanctuary. He's good with animals and gentle with his younger siblings. His sister, Tali, adores him. Also, I'm about ninety-five percent sure that he's not a murderer."

"You really need to let that go." Henry sighed and opened the gate, moving to help Sam with the goats. "And I'm two hundred percent sure he's not a murderer."

He thought back to the hour he'd spent talking with the young alpha. Tomás was in his early twenties, big and well built, with close cropped black hair and sparkling dark eyes. Yeah, he was handsome, but Sam was right. Tomás was also *kind*. He had listened to Henry ramble on about ridiculous things and simply encouraged him.

"He's going to make a coop for Sophie," Henry said, tugging at Goaty McGoatface. "He also liked the idea of having a grooming station in my mudroom. He's letting me style Mitzy, his Havanese-mix, too."

"You could do that professionally, you know." Sam darted away from Popcorn. "No, you just let go. Get!"

Goaty McGoatface finally let go of Sam, but Henry felt a tug and looked down. Tin Can had latched on to the pocket of his jeans. "Oh no."

The goats circled Henry and Sam, bleating softly as they nibbled at their clothes.

"We're surrounded." Sam sighed. "I left my phone inside."

"I left mine in Journey's pooch pouch." Henry shook his leg, but Goatzilla had latched on tight. "I shouldn't have left him with Aunt Mia."

"It's alright. I have my phone," Teague called from outside the stall. He held his phone up, clearly videoing their distress. "This is going on our social media for sure."

"Don't just stand there," Sam said, glaring at his husband. "Grab the treats and save us before they decide we're edible."

It took half an hour and a bag of treats, but eventually, the goats were distracted enough to let them flee with their clothes intact. Mostly.

Teague hadn't stopped laughing since he'd first seen them. "You always have to remember to bring the treats in with you."

"Haha, laugh it up, asshole." Sam hugged Teague. "You're back early."

"A woman called to arrange a drop off, so I came home right after the surgery."

"Is it a goat?" Henry asked. The sanctuary received a lot of farm animals. Some had health problems their owners couldn't cope with and others turned out to be more work than their humans expected. Either way, goats were a common drop off here. With Teague's skills, they were even able to rehome a lot of them, but they still had a barn full of goats.

Teague winced. "No goat. Columbo is an elderly scarlet Macaw parrot and belonged to the woman's grandfather who just passed away. She tried to keep him with her family, but it didn't work."

"Why not?" Sam asked.

"He's old, irritable, and curses. This one is probably going to be a lifetime resident."

Henry frowned. Not many people wanted a pet that wasn't cute and cuddly. Birds were harder to rehome in general, but one that would need that much care? Teague was right. No one would want him.

"He'll stay with us in the house, right?" Henry bit his lip. "He can stay in my room."

Teague shook his head. "We need to keep him quarantined until I check him over. We'll see after that. Being in a house with as many pets as we have may be more stress than he can handle."

Outside, the sun was getting low and the rain had picked up.

Sam slid in a patch of icy mud. "We need to re-gravel the walkways again. Damn it."

Henry sniffed. "I've already arranged for the walkways to be paved. I made an appointment for next month."

"That's too much money." Teague shook his head. "Your dad has already given us more than enough help."

"*Our* dad," Henry corrected. "And this is my money, not Dad's. Well, it's Grandfather's, but it's from *my* trust fund. I can spend it how I like."

Sam's boot sunk into the mud covering the path in front of them. "I vote we thank Henry and move on."

Teague growled. "I don't want to take advantage of you, Henry."

"I'm not a fool," Henry said, hurt. "Yes, I may mismanage my money sometimes, but I'm not stupid enough to spend it on someone who doesn't deserve it."

"We don't need it," Teague said, shaking his head. "You shouldn't worry about us."

"Seriously?" Sam gave them an exasperated look. "Teague, Henry is part of our family too. He lives and works here, so let him help when he wants to. Henry, no one here thinks you're stupid. We love you for the sweet baby bumblebee that you are."

"You've been talking with Audrey." Henry winced. "Shit."

Sam ruffled Henry's hair, making him huff. "Yes, I have. Now, Teague just needs to get used to accepting help from his family. Remember, he only had his dad to rely on for most of his life. Now, there's all of us. It may take him some time."

Teague sighed. "Why do you have to make so much sense?"

"Because I'm very sensible." Sam linked his arm with Henry's. "Let's go see get ready for the incoming bird."

By the time they reached the house, a blue minivan was parked in the driveway. A short, blond woman slammed the door behind her as she got out.

"Fuck off!" Columbo's squawks and curses were loud enough to wake the dead.

The woman closed her eyes, expression pained. "All day and all night. Please take this bird before I murder it."

Henry hurried around to the back of the van. Through the window, he could see Columbo. His feathers were dull and missing in places. He looked ragged, exhausted, and very unhappy.

"Fuck off," Columbo squawked again, head bobbing aggressively.

"Hey, handsome," Henry crooned. "It's going to be alright."

Sam led the woman to the house to fill out paperwork while Teague and Henry carried the bird and his large cage to one of the smaller barns.

"I have a space set up for him next to the exam room," Teague said, grunting as Columbo flapped around, unbalancing his cage.

"Poor guy." Henry huffed as they settled the cage in the exam room. "What can I do to help?"

Teague smiled softly. "You're a good person, Henry. You know that?"

His cheeks heated as he blushed. "I'll go check if she brought food for him."

"Umhm." Teague studied Columbo, then began to gather the tools he would need for the exam. "One day, you won't run away when I compliment you."

"Sure, and one day you won't hesitate to accept my help." Henry left the room, flustered. It was easy with Sam. They understood one another and were friends. Teague was different. With Henry and his family, Teague was like an unhappy hedgehog most of the time, all his quills up for defense. He still had that soft underbelly, though, and Henry had seen it more than once.

"Fuck, I've been spending too much time with the animals." He rubbed his face. "Get it together."

Memories of a handsome face and a soft voice made him sigh. He bet that Tomás would have known what to say to put everyone at ease. The young alpha had such a calm sense about him.

"HE HAS CATARACTS, osteoarthritis, and a case of candidiasis." Teague helped Henry settle Columbo's cage onto the table in front of the window of his new temporary home. It was just an empty storage closet next to the exam room, but it had a window and was quiet.

The poor bird looked miserable. "Fuck off."

"I think that's all he can say." Teague chuckled. "I don't blame him, though. He's been through a lot and is in pain."

"What does he need?" Henry asked, shifting from foot to foot.

"Medications will clear up his infection, but honestly, he needs a stable home." Teague looked around the room. "Not a storage closet. However, what we can give him is a nutritious, balanced diet and a clean environment."

"I'll take care of him and make sure he gets some exercise every day," Henry said, nibbling his lip. "Do you think anyone will adopt him?"

Teague shook his head. "Probably not. With a little time,

he might be able to handle some company. Bring Journey with you when you visit him, alright? He's good with the older animals. I don't think Columbo will ever be comfortable enough to stay in our living room with all our animals, but maybe we can fix up one of the rooms for him."

Henry studied the parrot. "I have to make a call. I'll check on him before I go to bet tonight."

"Okay." Teague rolled his shoulders and stretched his arms over his head. "I'll go feed the critters."

A few minutes later, Henry smiled as he dialed the number Tomás had given him earlier in the day.

"Hello?" Tomás answered on the second ring. Henry could hear several people talking in the background, the clink of dishes, and the occasional bark or meow of a pet.

"This is Henry Powell. Is this a bad time?" Henry asked, chewing at his thumbnail. It was a bad habit of his, but he couldn't make himself stop.

"Not at all. How are you, Henry?" Tomás's warm voice sent shivers down Henry's back.

"Okay, but there's been a development."

"What's going on?"

"There's this parrot named Columbo that we just took in. He needs a nice, peaceful home and lots of love. I can give him that, right? I'm going to introduce him to Journey tomorrow and see how it goes, but there's room at my house, isn't there? I can give him lots of space and attention. He has arthritis and cataracts and an infection, but we're going to treat the infection."

"Hey, remember to breathe," Tomás said, chuckling. "You can absolutely be there for Columbo. If he gets along with Journey, we can make him an area in your living room, right next to the windows. If not, you have a lot of space upstairs. We'll figure it out. Plus, I'm sure there are cage designs out there for older parrots. I'll look some up tonight. Do you want to meet for lunch tomorrow? We can talk it over."

"Are you sure you have time? I don't want to be a bother."

"I have plenty of time, and you'd never be a bother, Henry." Tomás's voice was full of smiles and sunshine, warming Henry. "This just gives me an excuse to talk with you more."

Henry flushed, then looked around, making sure no one saw that. "Thank you. Columbo isn't pretty or nice and that's what people want. You know? Just because he's not perfect doesn't mean he doesn't deserve a home."

"You're right. The old fella deserves love."

Henry sighed. "You get it. That's why I like you so much. Okay, so I'll see you tomorrow. Just text me the time and place."

"Will do. Now, tell me more about Columbo."

Henry grinned. "He talks big, but I can tell he's a sweetheart."

"I know a few of those. Remind me to introduce you to my friend Juan."

# TOMÁS

"Should we help him?" Juan asked, sledgehammer slung over his shoulder. "He did come in two hours early."

"Hmm, I'm not sure." Carter grabbed Tomás's thermos of coffee from where it sat on the hood of his truck. "He's the one that promised to build a chicken coop during mud season."

Tomás ignored them and slowly trudged through the mud to bring another load of rough lumber to the old wood-shed behind Henry's farmhouse. It was the closest outbuilding to the house and Tomás figured Henry would want Sophie's coop as close as possible. The walls were rotted in areas and there wasn't a floor, but Henry had some good ideas on how to make it look good.

"He won't even walk through the grass because he doesn't want it to turn into a mud pit."

Carter drank Tomás's coffee. "We can't interfere. We wouldn't want to upset his mating dance."

"Huh?" Juan tilted his head.

"You haven't met Henry yet," Carter said. "He's young and

handsome."

"Tomás wouldn't just fall for a nice face." Juan huffed. "Give the kid some credit."

"You're right." Carter took another drink. "Well, Henry also loves animals."

"That's better, but still," Juan shook his head, "I'm not convinced."

"Why else would he do this?" Carter waved toward him. "Look at him. He's gonna lose a boot in that shit."

Tomás trudged back to the truck for another load. "Will you two shut up? Either come help me or get back to knocking down walls. And leave my coffee alone, Carter. Zoe makes that special for me."

"Is he the boss now?" Juan asked, brow raised.

Carter laughed. "Don't worry. He knows I'm in charge."

"Wait, you're in charge?" Juan looked surprised.

"I'm the one who started the company, so of course I'm in charge."

"No way. I bring more to the company, so I'm obviously the boss," Juan countered.

Tomás came to a stop in the mud and glared at the two men. "Listen, assholes. I want at least a third of the walls on the first floor down before lunch. Don't make me call Gramps."

"Do you hear this?" Juan asked, giving Carter a disbelieving look.

Carter shrugged. "I told you. It's his mating dance. He's meeting Henry for lunch and wants to impress him."

"Threatening to call Gramps," Juan grumbled, shaking his head. "The nerve of some people."

Carter set Tomás's thermos down and pulled a few boards from the back of Tomás's truck. "Seriously. Like we'd be afraid of Gramps."

"There's one of him, but two of us." Juan grabbed some

boards as well and followed Carter through the mud. "What's there to be afraid of?"

Tomás smirked. They could bitch all they wanted, but they were properly motivated now.

A few hours later, Tomás had patched the walls of the shed and had almost finished framing the floor. He'd need to pick up some plywood in town after lunch, but he had some spare vinyl flooring he'd squirreled away from a previous job. It'd make clean-up in Sophie's coop easy and keep pests out.

He checked his phone for the time, then hiked back through the muddy yard to the house.

Juan danced in place to the music blasting from his Bluetooth speaker, and swung his sledgehammer, breaking apart another piece of the wall in front of him.

Carter grinned when he saw Tomás and tugged his earbuds out. "Plaster on lathing is a bitch, but the walls are coming down."

He could picture what the house would look like pass the mess in front of them and hoped Henry would too. They'd made good progress for their first day, and Tomás thought he'd have the coop ready by the time he needed to start on the electrical.

"Wow, this looks so different already."

Tomás spun around. Henry stood at the front door, looking crisp and clean cut in tight jeans, a gray sweater, and a navy overcoat. A gray beanie was pulled low over his ears, covering most of his hair.

Journey watched them from the navy pooch pouch hanging from Henry's chest, a matching grey beanie pulled over his furry head. His tiny ears poked out of slits on the top of the hat.

"You're here," Tomás said, suddenly a little breathless.

Henry grinned and waved a thick folder at him. "I have

ideas for Columbo."

"Great." Tomás cleared his throat. "Uh, you know Carter, but this is my other friend, Juan."

Henry's bright smiled, dimmed, turning shy. "Hello. It's nice to see you both. Thank you for working so hard. I can already envision what this place will look like."

Juan paused his music and set the sledgehammer down. "It's going to be nice. What's this about Columbo?"

Tomás let Henry's voice flow over him as he explained to Juan and Carter about the new addition at the sanctuary. He studied Henry's boots, noting the new wear on the heel and the splatters of mud at the bottom of his designer jeans. He wanted to know how Henry spent his days, what made him smile so brightly.

"What do you think about adding a picture window right here where you want to put his cage?" Carter asked, waving toward the back wall. "It could take place of these two smaller windows."

"I love that idea." Henry patted Journey's side. "That will make it a little more entertaining for Columbo and Journey both."

"Where are you going for lunch?" Juan asked, giving Tomás an innocent look. "Maybe Carter and I can come."

Tomás glared at his friend. "You said you were meeting Jackson for lunch. Remember? Henry and I should go." He ignored Carter completely and took Henry's hand. "Have you been to Zoe's bakery, Honey Buns?"

"No, but Sam brought back some cinnamon rolls from there once. They were so good."

"She has a soup and sandwich special that I think you'll like." Tomás opened the truck door for Henry and shut it once he was seated. He really hoped the omega couldn't see the two idiots standing at the window staring at them with grins.

A short time later, they sat across from one another at Honey Buns, coffees in hand as they waited for their food. It was odd watching the people around him react to Henry. Normally, they would say hello to Tomás or at least nod at him when passing. With Henry there, most seemed reluctant to approach them. Henry seemed oblivious to the curious stares aimed toward him.

"Journey and I stayed with Columbo last night," Henry said, yawning. "I thought he might get scared, but all he did was sleep."

"Does he mind Journey?"

Henry shook his head, smiling softly. "Not at all. Journey doesn't bark much and is gentle with other animals. He just watched Columbo and woofed when the parrot talked."

"That's good."

"Do you think you can bring Mitzy by one day and see how he does with her?"

Tomás nodded. "Absolutely. She mostly sleeps all day while I'm gone, but I'm sure she could use the company."

Henry's phone vibrated on the table and the omega winced. "That's my sister again. She's convinced I need to add on to the house. She says I need a foyer, a coat room, and a formal dining room at the very least."

Tomás snorted. "Carter gets a lot of emails from her, but he keeps telling her that we can't change the plans unless you tell us too."

Henry sighed. "I love her, but I don't want a mini mansion. I just want my Victorian farmhouse."

"It can be hard telling family, no." Tomás winced, understanding his frustration. "My little sister, Tali, is convinced I need to do something, but I really don't want to. I tell her no, but she thinks she knows better than me."

"What does she want you to do?"

"Did Gramps tell you I was adopted?" Tomás couldn't

believe he was having this conversation on a first maybe-date, but Henry was easy to talk to.

"He said your parents, Marco and Bennett, adopted you a few years ago, right before you graduated high school."

"Yeah." Tomás laughed, shaking his head. "It surprised the hell of me, but I'm glad they're my parents. My biological dad is doing a life sentence at Riverbend in Nashville, Tennessee. My biological mom was in prison too, but she was released early about a month ago. She reached out and wants to meet up."

"Tali thinks you should?" Henry asked, reaching across the table to hold his hand.

Tomás nodded. "Yeah, but I don't want to. When I was growing up, I knew I was missing something other kids had, but I didn't really understand it. My life had always been solitary. It was just how it was, so I dealt with it. Maybe, if she had reached out then, I would have wanted to talk with her."

"What changed?"

"Marco and Bennett Wilson." Tomás smiled softly. "My dads showed me what family means. It's not conditional, and it doesn't end when you're a legal adult. It's about love and loyalty. Family are people who stand with you during life. Who will listen to you and care about you. It's like there's this invisible thread that connects us all together. Threads that they helped create. They're a part of who I am – my memories, my personality and values, all of that. My biological mom and I don't have that bond. We never did."

"That's beautiful," Henry whispered, looking thoughtful.

Tomás flushed. "Yeah, sorry about that. I didn't mean to get all philosophical."

"Never apologize for knowing what family means." Henry's laugh hurt Tomás's heart. "I can name my ancestors through fourteen generations on Papa's side and sixteen generations on Dad's side. To me, family has always been the Powell name. This huge boulder of expectation that hangs around my neck. I like your definition much better than mine."

Tomás squeezed Henry's hand, not knowing the right words to comfort the omega.

"Cinnamon rolls on the house." Zoe set a plate of the bakery's specialty between them, then leaned over to kiss the top of Tomás's head. "For my sweet, little cousin."

Tomás kept staring at Henry, silently begging the omega to ignore the woman cooing over him like a damn dove.

Henry snickered, betraying him.

"By the way, it's nice to finally meet you, Henry." Zoe plopped onto the seat beside him. "Sam talks about you all the time, and we've all seen you from a distance. Please come visit us more. I'll give you all the sweets you can eat."

Henry bit his lip, eying the rolls. "These smell delicious. Papa would disapprove, but I don't care. I'm going to eat two."

"Well now, that just makes me want to feed you more." Zoe stood and pressed a kiss to Henry's forehead, making him startle. "You boys enjoy your date and remember that I'm a goddess for pretending not to notice the dog zipped up in your coat despite our *no pets* policy."

"Date?" Henry squeaked, mouth full of cinnamon roll. He absently patted the lump that was Journey.

Tomás glared at his cousin as she walked away, hips swinging. "Ignore her. It's only a date if you want it to be a date. Otherwise, this is just two friends having lunch."

Henry turned an interesting shade of red. "I haven't been on a date in a while. Is it going alright?"

Tomás let the omega's words sink in and shivered. "It's definitely going well."

"Then, he invited me to his house for dinner," Henry said, smiling.

"Fuck off." Columbo slowly lumbered down the padded ramp leading from his cage and hopped onto the low, fleece wrapped perch next to Henry's chair.

"Normally, I'm a mess before a first date. Well, any date really. I have to find the perfect outfit and style my hair just right." Henry leaned down and gave Columbo a treat. This was the first time the parrot had come out of his cage. "Now, I'm not nervous at all. I'm excited to see Tomás and get to know more about him. That's all. Isn't it amazing?"

Journey looked up from where he lay on the dog bed next to the perch and woofed softly.

"Fuck off."

"Woof."

"Fuck off."

"Woof."

"Journey Alexander Powell, you better be nice to your new brother." Henry gave Columbo another treat. "That rule applies to you too, Christopher Columbo Powell. Family stands together. That's what Tomás says."

"Here you are." Sam closed the door softly, staying a distance away from Columbo so he wouldn't startle the parrot. Casey gurgled happily from where he was nestled in his baby sling.

"That's Sam and Casey," Henry told Columbo. "They're family too, so be nice."

"Fuck off."

"Woof."

Sam grinned. "Your new house won't be quiet."

"Nope." Henry didn't mind it in the least either. "How was work?"

"Good. I'm happy to be working with Rueben again. The evening shift isn't bad, but dayshift is better." Sam lowered himself to the floor, folding his legs under him. "What time are you going to Tomás's?"

"In a couple of hours. I want to help with the evening chores first."

Sam leaned back against the wall. "Teague had an idea and I fully, one hundred percent support it."

"What is it?" Henry fed Columbo another treat since he was such a good boy.

"We want to include your name on the sanctuary too. As an owner with all the authority and responsibility that goes with that."

Henry froze in place, hand in front of Columbo. "What?"

"Right now, everything is set up with Teague and I as the owners, but you're as much a part of this as we are. Teague is able to take in more animals, because we know we can rely on your help with the daily chores. Hell, you do more than I do."

"You have a full-time job and a newborn," Henry pointed out. "You do more than anyone would expect you to."

"That's all the more reason we need you."

Henry thought for a moment. "I do have money I could put into the sanctuary."

Sam rolled his eyes. "That's not the point. We want *you*. Not your money."

"Are you high?" Henry side-eyed Sam. "I'm just me. I don't have an education or experience. Nothing worthwhile."

"You helped us when you didn't have to." Sam slid a little closer to them. "You have such a love for all the critters that end up here. That's the absolute most important thing."

A sudden weight on his wrist, made him jump. Columbo scooted awkwardly to his forearm.

"Fuck off." The parrot studied him, head tilted.

"Woof." Journey grinned at them, tongue hanging out.

Sam chuckled. "Perfect timing, Columbo. See what I mean, baby bumblebee? We all need you here. What do you say?"

Henry closed his eyes, savoring the moment. Sam and Teague needed *him*. They didn't need just anyone. They needed him. Henry Powell. Teague trusted him with his dream. It was frightening, but damn, his soul needed to hear those words.

"Are you sure? Remember, you had to teach me how to make a monthly budget. Do you really trust me?"

"We do." Sam patted Casey's back. "I told Teague he needed to be the one to ask, but I swear the two of you are experts at dancing around one another."

Henry winced. "Yeah, we don't really talk."

"So how about it?"

The joy building in him was completely unfamiliar. Usually, a responsibility like this would have him running away to one of his favorite resorts, desperate to escape the expectations. That's what he'd done when his eldest brother, Sterling, had wanted him to work at their father's company.

*I can do this*, he thought, amazed. *I help them every day and they trust me.*

"If you're really sure about it, then yes." Henry fed Columbo a treat and watched the bird bob his head. "It's important to help the animals no one wants. They need love too."

*We all do.*

Tomás's house was a short drive from where Sam and Teague lived. The small cabin was surrounded by trees, a little red barn, and fenced pasture. Neat flowerbeds lined the steps and walkway leading to the front door. Henry didn't know what kind of flowers they were, but he thought they'd be pretty when blooming. They'd have to be because Tomás had planted them.

"Hey." Tomás leaned against the doorframe dressed in jeans and a loose, long-sleeved shirt. A small dog with white fur danced around his bare feet.

"Hi," Henry ducked his head and focused on the dog. "This must be Mitzy."

"Yeah, she's good with other animals if you think Journey may want to play with her." Tomás

Journey woofed from the pooch pouch Henry wore.

Mitzy froze in her dance, sat on her haunches, and gave Journey a sweet look.

"Do you want to play?" Henry asked, pulling his dog from the pouch. The Pomeranian wore a blue and white sweater to match the occasion.

The two dogs sniffed one another a few times, then trotted off into the house.

"I'll take that as a yes," Henry said, shrugging.

"Come on in. Dinner is almost ready. I made chicken parmesan with gnocci. It's the nicest meal Papa taught me to make."

"It sounds delicious." Henry looked around. "Your house is so cute."

Tomás's cabin was neat and cozy, decorated in warm tones with oversized furniture. There were a lot more live plants than Henry had expected. He eyed an especially large fern that sat next to the couch.

Tomás sighed. "It's too many plants, isn't it? My cousins, Janelle and Zed, are plant lovers and keep bringing me cuttings from their favorites. I don't have the heart to tell them I don't really want any more plants."

Henry covered his mouth, trying not to laugh at the flustered alpha.

"If you think that's bad, look at this." Tomás opened a closet next to the front door. It was full of knitted scarves, sweaters, and caps. Some were done beautifully, but others were complete disasters. "My cousin Ernie is a knitter and is pretty good, but my brother-in-law, Grey, is a mess. They have this whole knitting war going on, so if one of them gifts me something, the other thinks he has to outdo him."

Henry couldn't hold back his laughter anymore.

"Laugh all you want, but remember, all I have to do is mention you to Papa, and the Wilsons will be all over you. You'll have more plants, baked goods, and scarves than you can handle."

Henry snickered. "They just love you."

"They do." Tomás shook his head. "I'm still not used to it. One moment, I'm living in a homeless shelter, trying to find enough to eat, and the next, I have a family and home."

"That had to be a big change."

"It was." Tomás led him to the kitchen. A pot bubbled on

the oven, the scent of tomato pasta filling the air. "Have a seat while I finish cooking. There's some wine on the table."

Henry sat down and studied the bottle of wine. It was locally made on an apple orchard. *From another of his Wilson cousins*, Henry thought, smiling.

"Things are better now," Tomás continued. "I think I could have survived on my own, but Dad and Papa have taught me the difference between surviving and living. I have a good job and a home I own, but growing up the way I did gives me some perspective. I know what's important in life. What will make me happy."

"You're ahead of me. I'm twenty-six and only now figuring out what actually makes me happy."

Tomás pulled on oven mitts and took a pan from the oven. "Nothing wrong with that. Some lessons take longer to learn."

"I like that thought." Henry propped his chin on his fist and enjoyed the sight of Tomás moving around the kitchen. "Do you like where you are, working with Carter and Juan?"

"Oh yeah." Tomás looked over his shoulder, grinning. "They're good friends, and they've taught me a lot. I enjoy helping people and this way I can get paid to do it."

Henry nodded. "I can see the draw of that."

"What about you?" Tomás asked. "Did you always want to work at an animal sanctuary?"

"God no," Henry said, snorting a laugh. He closed his eyes, embarrassed at the sound. Hopefully, Tomás hadn't noticed. "My omega father, we call him papa too, he raised us with certain expectations."

"What were they?"

"To be a Powell is to be perfect." Henry closed his eyes. "Stay composed, don't complain, don't cause a scene. That wasn't enough though. We needed to be *more* than everyone else too. More attractive, more successful. Wear the most fashionable clothing, have all the right hobbies, and socialize with the right people. People from an *approved* family. Then, we needed to go to the most prestigious university, have the best grades, and work to make the family company even more successful. After we've accomplished all of that, we need to marry the spouse chosen for us from one of the other wealthy families in our social circle and carry on our family name."

Tomás stared at him, amazed. "Wow. That's a lot of expectations."

Henry snorted again. "It really is. Audrey and I both failed horribly at it too. Papa gets so mad at us." He shook his head. "I can't complain, though. I've never struggled like you. Dad made millions at his company, and Grandfather left all of us trust funds."

Tomás hummed and stirred the sauce. "Money is nice. It's only easy to say you don't need it when you have it."

"People will do insane things to keep it too." Henry shivered. "Money and power. Back in New York... No, never mind. It's really not so horrible."

Tomás moved to the table and leaned over Henry. "One thing I know for sure is that personal trauma comes in all shapes and sizes. Having money doesn't change that. Please don't minimize your hurt just because you think you've had it easier. Pain isn't a competition."

Henry narrowed his eyes. "How did you get so wise?"

"Learned it from Mitzy." Tomás grinned.

Henry couldn't resist the alpha's smile. He leaned forward and pressed his lips to Tomás's. The instant they touched, the world faded away until the only thing left was the warmth of the kiss, the unsteady thumping of his heartbeat, and Tomás's sweet scent.

This wasn't normal. Kissing never made Henry lose his

mind. He could only hold the thought for a moment before it disappeared along with his reason.

The alpha's hands cupped the back of Henry's head, holding him still as he deepened the kiss, his tongue sliding against Henry's. Fire bubbled inside him, slowly building and spreading through his body.

It had been so long since someone touched him and it had never felt like this. Tomás's touch was reverent, making Henry feel fragile and precious.

Eventually, Tomás pulled away, breaking the kiss with a low moan. Henry watched him in a daze, body burning hotter than it ever had.

"You are addictive." Tomás stood straight, eyes flaming with need. "Pour me a glass of wine?"

"Sure," Henry said, voice raspy. Hands trembling, he grabbed the bottle of wine. "It's, um, been a while for me, and my last relationship was a mess. Well, *every* relationship I've had has been a mess. What about you?"

Tomás shrugged and took the glass Henry offered. "I've dated a bit, but never anything serious." His dark eyes heated as he stared at Henry. "Never met anyone I was interested in. Until now."

"Hmm." Henry sipped his wine, hiding his pleased smile. "That's good to know."

A few moments later, Tomás set a steaming plate in front of him. "When I moved here, all I could do was focus on adjusting to suddenly having a family, people who cared about me. There wasn't room for anything else. It's been a few years now, and I'm in a good place. You… there's something about you I need."

Henry swallowed hard. "You make me feel like I'm something special. I don't want to disappoint you, but I'm just me. Completely useless except for my money."

Tomás's eyes narrowed. "Someone made you feel that

way, maybe a lot of someones, but I think you know it's not true."

Henry sat, quiet and flustered, looking around the cozy kitchen for a moment, gaze finally latching onto the calm and steady alpha sitting across from him, eyes gentle and knowing.

"I don't understand you," Henry said, voice breaking. "You're strong, handsome, and smart with a million people that care about you. Fuck, you're self-aware and empowered at what? Twenty-one?"

"Twenty-two."

"Oh, twenty-two. Yeah, that makes a difference." Henry rolled his eyes. "Why would you want to spend time with someone like me?"

"I don't need a reason." Tomás reached across the table and laid his hand over Henry's. "Listen, some wounds take longer to heal than others. I've felt useless before, stupid and unlovable. It took some time to change that. Don't beat yourself up."

"Your family helped you." Henry pulled his hand away. "Is that why you want to help me? To pay it forward?"

Tomás smirked. "Yeah, I'm not that selfless. First of all, you don't need me to learn how to accept and love yourself. Only you can do that. Second, I want to be the one beside you. To spend time with you, get to know you. Maybe I'm meant to be your person and you, mine. Plus, I'd really like to fuck you. That's definitely not selfless."

Henry laughed hard enough to snort again. "You have such a way with words."

Tomás nodded solemnly. "It's a gift and a curse."

"Teague and Sam are going to make me a partner in the sanctuary," he blurted out. "They trust me. This is Teague's dream and he wants *me* to be a part of it."

Tomás's smile grew. "And you think you're useless? Clearly bullshit."

"Maybe you're right."

"Now, how about we eat dinner, then go play with the dogs?"

Henry grinned, feeling light as air. "Best date ever."

# TOMÁS

A couple of weeks later, Tomás sat on the floor of Columbo's room and watched Henry bottle feed puppies. This was his favorite way of watching the omega. Henry was so confident when he was with animals, his smile natural and beautiful.

They'd met up every night since their first date, sometimes eating dinner at Tomás's house and sometimes with Aunt Mia and the others. He hadn't lied to Henry when he'd told him he wanted to spend time with him. Tomás didn't want to be away from his omega for even a moment. Which was why he was spending his lunch break at the sanctuary.

It was a cozy lunch, at least. Mitzy and Journey slept curled in a dog bed next to Columbo's cage while the parrot perched on a stand near Henry. His omega's chicken, Sophie, sat near the dogs, gently pecking the bedding. Aunt Mia had even brought them sandwiches.

"The girl who brought the puppies in said her dad was going to throw them in the lake." Henry looked up, eyes full of anger. "I'd like to put him in a bag and throw him in a cold lake to see how he likes it."

Tomás nodded, petting the little pup he was feeding. It was teeny tiny with white fur and a pink nose. "I'll help you."

"She said he told her that their dog had too many puppies to take care of." Henry gently placed the puppy he held back in the padded laundry basket with the other puppies and took another out to feed. "That doesn't justify killing some of the puppies. If mama dog can't care for all her puppies, then it's the human's responsibility to help."

"How many did she have?" Tomás peeked into the basket and counted. There were ten puppies counting the two they were feeding.

"Twenty-two."

"Whoa, that's a lot."

"They're Great Pyrenees. The girl said their dog usually has a large litter once a year, but had never had one this big before. They raise the pups to sell as livestock guardians."

"You'd think he'd want to keep all the puppies he could if he's making money from them."

Henry winced. "Well, they need to be fed every two hours."

"I see." Tomás traded his puppy in for the next hungry baby. "Are you taking care of them yourself?"

"During the day Teague and I are alternating feedings. At night, there are four of us alternating, so it's easier. We did the same when Casey was first born."

"I have the feeling that Dad is getting two livestock guardians when these babies are old enough." Tomás chuckled as the pup in his hand burped, dribbling milk.

"Mitzy told me she wants a little sister too." Henry gave him a sweet look. "The one in your hands is a girl."

Tomás groaned. "That's not fair. I can't say no when you look at me like that."

Henry grinned. "That's the point."

"It's what I get for dating a handsome man that works at an animal sanctuary."

"We're dating?" Henry's cheeks turned red. "I wasn't sure, since you didn't say anything. Did I tell you it's been a while since my last relationship?"

"A few times." Tomás leaned over and kissed Henry. "Yes, we're dating. You and me. No one else allowed."

"Fuck off." Columbo hopped off his perch and slowly made his way up the ramp into his cage.

"Woof." Journey's ear twitched.

"Woof." Mitzy raised her head, looking around.

"Fuck off."

"Woof."

"Woof."

"Oh no." Tomás shared a look with Henry as he lowered the puppy back into the basket. "Now Mitzy's doing it too."

"Fuck off."

"Woof."

"Woof."

"That's the last puppy." Henry settled his own puppy in with the others. "Soon, Sophie and all the puppies will be talking back to Columbo too."

Tomás held his arms open, and the omega crawled over to lay against him, sighing happily when the Tomás's arms closed around him. He rested his chin on top of the omega's head.

"Why do you call him Christopher Columbo?" Tomás asked, tightening his arms around Henry.

"Christopher Columbus is an explorer, right? That's who he's named after."

"I thought he was named after that old show, *Columbo*."

"Huh?"

"You don't know about *Columbo*? It was popular in the seventies."

Henry side eyed him. "How do you know about it? You're younger than me."

"One of the few memories I have of my abuelo is watching reruns of the show with him. I don't even remember what's it's about. I just remember sitting on his lap and trying not to fall asleep so I could spend more time with him."

"How long did you have him?" Henry asked, voice full of tenderness.

"Until I was five. Abuelo and Abuela died in a car accident, I went into foster care."

"Fuck off."

"Woof."

"Woof."

"Bad timing, guys," Henry mumbled, making Tomás laugh.

"To be honest, he reminds me of Abuelo, grumpy on the outside, and tired and in pain on the inside. Still sweet though."

Henry laughed. "I think we need to watch *Columbo*. What was it about again?"

Tomás shrugged. "An old guy named Columbo."

"Yeah, we need to watch it. Tonight?"

"Sure. The only night I can't be with you this week is Saturday. My younger siblings are coming over for a movie night sleep over. We watch movies and they camp out in the living room all night."

"It's great you like spending time with them." Henry leaned back against him. "Audrey and I spent time together since we're close in age, but Sterling didn't know what to do with us. You should see him try to comfort one of us when we're upset. He's all awkward hugs and weird head pats."

"They won't let me be awkward." Tomás grinned. "Half

the time, they're the ones making sure I *feel loved*. Like I'm the only one at prom without a date, so I need all their support. If I didn't like you so much, I'd make you come too. They'd be all over you. Hannah and Drew are home from college on spring break, so it'll be them, Tali, Terry, and Nate."

Henry leaned back and cupped Tomás's face. "Aww, you're such a good big brother. What are you watching?"

"All the Shrek movies since Nate is just five. It was that or *Frozen* and *Frozen II* for the hundredth time. Those were the only options I was given."

Henry chuckled. "Enjoy it. Didn't you say Tali was graduating high school this year? Then she'll go off to college too and you'll only have Terry and Nate to sleep over with their big brother."

Tomás winced. "Tali and college are not topics you want to bring up together right now."

"Uh-oh."

"Papa and Dad want her to at least try college, but she has her heart set on running the ranch with Dad."

"Can't she take classes online and do both?" Henry asked.

"She could, but they want her to have the whole college experience. Honestly, Tali knows what she wants. There's no point in trying to change her mind. Plus, Dad loves working with her. I think it's mostly Papa that worries about it."

Henry frowned. "Are they really disappointed in her?"

Tomás leaned down and kissed Henry softly. "Not at all. They'll accept and support her decision in the end. They just have to work through it first."

"Good. Papa was furious when I refused to go to college. He didn't talk to me for months. Dad didn't say anything. It was like he knew I wasn't good enough anyway."

Tomás scowled. His omegas parents had done a number

on him, knowingly or not. "I'm sure you would have been just fine if you chose to go."

"Sterling and Audrey graduated top of their classes." Henry pressed his cheek to Tomás's chest. "I wouldn't have been able to do that."

"All you can do is be the best you. You don't have to compete with anyone."

Henry looked up with a slight smile. "Thanks for that. What about you? Did you want to go to college?"

"Nope." Tomás shook his head. "Almost joined the Navy but decided to train with Carter. Started out plumbing, but I like electrical work better. Speaking of, your house is completely rewired. Plumbing's finished too. New walls are up. The AC/heating unit is going in tomorrow."

"You all work fast." Henry gave him an excited look. "Can I see it tonight or do I need to stay out of the way?"

"Come by tonight. I'll keep the heaters running so you and Journey don't freeze."

"You'll be there?"

"I'll even bring dinner."

A short time later, Tomás left Henry with the animals and drove the short distance back to the farm house. Juan was already back to work installing the new windows, he danced around, Bluetooth speaker blaring Dolly Parton. The other alpha was an odd one.

Juan tightened a screw in the window frame. "Little Tomás is late. Did you have trouble pulling yourself away from your omega?"

Tomás grinned. "You're lucky I came back at all. If I could, I'd just follow him around all day."

"Aww, you're so cute." Juan grinned. "When are you going to tell your papa that you're in love?"

"It's too soon for love." Tomás changed the music from "White Limousine" to Neil Young's "Revolution Blues."

"Your face says different."

"I didn't say I wasn't in love. It's just too soon to tell anyone." He picked up the handles of the sander. "He's it. I don't know why or how, but I know he's it for me."

"It happens like that for some people. Especially Wilsons." Juan changed the music back to Dolly. "Baby I'm Burnin'" started playing loudly. "You're too young to listen to Neil Young. What's wrong with you?"

"Dolly Parton is any better?" Tomás switched the playlist back to Neil Young, choosing "Old Man" this time. "Papa loves Neil Young and raised me right. This is the way."

"You two are ridiculous." Carter shut the door behind him. "I can't escape Dolly or Neil. This is why I have earbuds."

"Our baby boy is in *lurve*." Juan wrapped an arm around Tomás's shoulders. "Look at that blush."

Carter winced. "I know. Zoe spread the word after seeing you with him. She tried to hold it in, but she couldn't take it. By now, all the Wilsons know you're in love."

"Damn it." Tomás scowled. "How did Zoe know? I didn't even know until yesterday. They better not scare Henry off. He has things to work through, and I plan on being there beside him as he does."

"It does no good to worry about what the Wilsons will do." Juan ruffled his hair, then went back to setting the window. "They're going to do what they're going to do. There's no stopping them. Like an ocean of meddling and good intentions. It'll drag you under eventually."

"Elijah said Ernie was already knitting him something and Janelle is repotting some houseplants to bring over." Carter gave him a sympathetic look. "Since you can't fight them, join them. Use the family. Elijah sent a crate of wine to work with me. He said something about Reuben cooking you a romantic meal. I don't know."

"Damn it," Tomás turned the sander on. He still had a lot of the floor to cover and Sophie's coop wasn't quite finished. "Wait." He stopped and looked at Carter. "You said to use the family, right?"

# HENRY

Henry parked Teague's truck outside of the farmhouse and waved at Tomás. The alpha waited for him on the sagging front porch.

"Are you two ready?" he asked, looking down at the dapper pups strapped into the seat next to him.

"Woof." Journey grinned at him, proud of his tuxedo coat and black bowtie.

Mitzy pouted next to him, clearly not excited about the black tulle skirt and silk hairbows Henry and Teague had dressed her in.

"You look beautiful, Mitzy. Dates are a chance to show off your looks."

Tomás opened his door. "Are you coming?"

Henry handed Mitzy to him. "We're coming."

"Wow, you look good, sweetheart."

"Sadly, I know you're talking to Mitzy."

Tomás winced. "You look even better. Um, sweetheart."

Henry chuckled and handed Journey to him as well. "Good save."

Truthfully, Tomás was the handsome one today. The alpha was all cleaned up and dressed in nice slacks and a dress shirt.

"You look really nice too," Henry said, cheeks heating.

"Thanks." Tomás grinned. "Come inside. I have a surprise for you."

Henry hurried out of the truck and up the steps to the front door. "I can't wait to see how different it is."

"Just keep in mind, we have a long way to go."

Henry gasped when he went inside. The whole downstairs space was open and the floor was bare of carpet. Instead, lovely pinewood floors were on display, the grain of the wood prominent, each individual knot there for all to see. *Perfect imperfections.*

"The floor isn't quite done. There were a few pieces I needed to add in to fill in gaps. I can stain them to match the rest of the pine's natural patina. Plus, I still need to sand it again and add a coat of poly." Tomás froze in place. "Oh fuck. Do you hate it?"

"Hate it?" Henry barely noticed the tears running down his face. All he could see was the beauty Tomás had revealed to him. He knelt and ran a hand over one of the dark knots. "No ugly carpet covering it. No grime and dirt. All of this beauty was hidden away." He looked up at Tomás. "I couldn't love it more than I do now."

Tomás looked relieved. "Oh good. This isn't even your surprise."

Henry laughed, wiping away his tears. "What could possibly top this?"

"Well," Tomás said, drawing the word out. "Follow me."

Henry let Tomás pull him to the far side of the house, only then noticing the low, romantic lighting. In the corner of what would be the living room, a large picture window looked out over the backyard. Strands of fairy lights hung around the window and a gorgeous wooden coffee table sat in front of it, a large woven rug under it. Large, colorful pillows were arranged around the table and several healthy green plants sat in the center. Steam rose from the plates of food waiting for them.

"Coconut curry." Tomás helped him sit on a pillow, then followed him down. "Personally delivered from the Irish Rose."

"That's where Sam works." Henry sniffed the plate. "This is Rueban's curry, isn't it? I've always wanted to try it."

"Yep. He's the best cook in the world." Tomás patted the coffee table. "My brother Harper brought this over. He made it for you as a housewarming gift. My cousin Janelle brought the plants, and she said these are safe to have around pets. Papa brought the pillows and the rug." Harper pulled a folded, dark green blanket from under the table. "My cousin Ernie made this. He said to tell you it's a chunky cable knit blanket and if you want more, just let him know. He enjoys making them."

Henry looked around, eyes watering again. "This is the nicest thing anyone has ever done for me."

Tomás wrapped his arms around Henry. "I'm not done yet. Look out the window."

The sun was setting outside, but he could still see the solar lights lining a gravel and stone pathway leading from the house to a small outbuilding. The building was painted white, with cute windows and flowerboxes. A large maple tree grew above it, branches still bare from winter.

Henry jumped to his feet, startling Tomás and the dogs. "Is that Sophie's coop?"

Tomás laughed, standing up. "I guess you're not going to eat first, huh?"

Squealing, he ran out the back door and down the stone path. Snow melted from the tall grass and weeds growing on each side, making the ground wet and muddy. The pathway was nice and sturdy, held together with thick stone borders. It would be a huge boon in the winter.

As he grew closer, the chicken coop looked even better. The flowerboxes were empty since the weather was still too cold, but the maple tree had small red buds growing, telling the world that spring was here. A fenced in run was attached to the side, large enough for several chickens. *Sophie is going to be so spoiled*, he thought, grinning.

He opened the door and started laughing. An actual chandelier hung from the ceiling and lit up the building. It was small, a mixture of bronze metal and crystals of varying sizes. The floor was gray vinyl plank flooring, and the walls matched the outside. Two hen boxes sat against the back wall, full of straw and fragrant herbs. A heat lamp hung above them, light dim. Wide, flat boards were attached to the walls in one corner, low to ground so Sophie would be able to easily hop up to roost.

What surprised Henry the most was the large white brahma perched on one of the roosts, clucking softly.

"That's Clucky." Tomás leaned against his back and pulled him close. "She is the most chill chicken Papa has ever seen. He thought that you might like to introduce her to Sophie. I don't think she'll pick on her. The only chickens she doesn't like are roosters. She's kind to all the hens and new chicks in Papa's flock."

"She's precious." Henry wiped his eyes. "This is perfect for Sophie. That chandelier is so beautiful that I'm tempted to steal it for myself."

"You like it? I made it. I collect bits and pieces of everything. The flooring and the windows were left over from a project. I picked up the crystals at different shops over the past few years."

"You made the chandelier?" Henry spun around, staring at Tomás in wonder. "You made that?"

Tomás's cheeks turned red. "You really like it?"

"It's gorgeous."

Tomás scratched behind his ear, suddenly looking shy. "I'm working with Harper to make some to sell. Do you think you might like one inside your house?"

Henry groaned and hugged the alpha tight. "I'd love anything you make for me. You're pure magic, Tomás Wilson. Did you know that?"

"Only for you." Tomás whispered against his ear, nuzzling him.

Henry pulled him down for a kiss, savoring the feel and taste of his alpha. "No one has ever done something like this for me. Thank you."

"I really like your heart," Tomás said, pressing his forehead to Henry's. "You're kind and patient, but fiercely protective. You deserve all the good things in the world."

Henry's body shook, emotions overwhelming him. No one had ever described him like that. He was used to compliments but they weren't about his personality. He was known to be good-looking and fashionable. Pampered and wealthy. A pretty face and acceptable armpiece.

Tomás was different from anyone Henry had ever been with. He was so much better than Henry deserved.

Henry wrapped his arms around Tomás and kissed him again, almost frantic to connect with the amazing alpha in front of him.

"Inside," Tomás managed to say in between kisses. The alpha lifted Henry up and he quickly wrapped his legs around Tomás's waist. He was only vaguely away of the stumbling, slow trek back into the house. All he could think about was the sweet taste of his alpha and the hard abdomen pressed against his dick.

A moment later, the backdoor closed behind them and Tomás laid Henry gently on the mound of pillows surrounding the coffee table.

Henry tugged Tomás's shirt, pulling him down to lay alongside him. "This may be my dick talking, but I think I love you, Tomás."

The alpha laughed roughly, thumb sliding along Henry's bottom lip. "I love you too, sweetness."

Tomás kissed Henry, tightening his arms around him. Henry moaned and moved to straddle Tomás, his tongue sliding against his alpha's.

Tomás's fingers fumbled with the buttons of Henry's shirt. "So many buttons."

Henry leaned back and wiggled out of his pants and underwear. "Just rip it."

Tomás's warm hands ran up the sides of Henry's bare thighs, and he shuddered, dick hardening even more. He moved his hips against Tomás, feeling the alpha's erection pressing against his ass.

"Henry," Tomás said, breathless. "I need you."

Henry pulled his shirt off, ignoring the ripping sound and leaned in for another kiss. "Good."

Tomás growled and cupped Henry's ass as he arched up. He rubbed a finger against Henry's hole.

Henry shuddered. "Are you okay without a condom? I'm clean and on birth control."

"I'm clean too."

"Lube. Do we have lube?"

Tomás pressed a kiss to Henry's collarbone. "Under the table with the blanket. Ernie is my favorite cousin."

Henry leaned over and grabbed the small bottle next to the blanket. "He's my favorite too." A few minutes later, he gasped when Tomás's finger stretched his hole. He pushed back, moaning when Tomás added a second finger. "Ernie is the best."

"Stop talking about my cousin," Tomás said, smiling against Henry's neck. "I want your attention on me."

Henry unbuttoned Tomás's pants and hummed in appreciation as he took in the size of his dick. He squeezed some lube into his palm and slowly stroked Tomás, learning the shape and the feel of his alpha. "You have my complete attention, love."

Tomás rolled him onto the pillows and braced himself above him. "Good. This is my favorite part." Tomás held his gaze and slowly pushed into him.

Henry lost all ability to speak. Long, smooth strokes in and out of his ass took up all his attention until Tomás leaned down and kissed him again.

*I really do love him*, Henry thought, losing himself to the feel of their bodies moving together as Tomás wrapped him in his arms. He'd never felt so close to someone before and maybe he should have been afraid. It was Tomás, though. Henry would trust the alpha with his life.

Tomás hit just the right spot and Henry's thoughts scattered as he lost it, calling out his alpha's name and coming hard.

A few moments later, Tomás came, filling Henry's ass.

They lay together on the pillows, panting while they caught their breath. Henry's eyes met Journey's. The two dogs sat a short distance away, eyes wide as they stared at their humans.

"Uh-oh." Henry winced. "We may have shocked our fur babies."

Tomás sat up, groaning. "They'll live. They have to because I really want to do that again."

Henry wrapped the knitting blanket around them. "We

have food, a heater, and comfortable pillows. I think they're going to adjust to seeing us together."

Tomás grinned and kissed him. "They'll have a lot of practice."

Henry burrowed against him. "I have to text Sam, though. Otherwise, he'll think we got murdered."

The next morning, Henry sat on the back stoop of his house and watched the sun slowly rise. Juan's Bluetooth and MP3 player sat beside him, volume low, as he listened to Dolly Parton's "Light of a Clear Blue Morning."

He knew of Dolly, of course, everyone did, but he'd never heard her music before. The song spoke of dark nights ending and new days dawning. The beginning of hope and the certainty that the future would work itself out.

Henry felt the words deep inside him. In the past, after spending the night with a man, he'd be self-conscious, embarrassed at the idea of not meeting expectations. He'd worry about what his parents and friends would say about a new relationship. Would they approve? Would he be accepted by the boyfriend's friends and family? For years, he'd tried so hard to be the perfect son, the perfect boyfriend, the perfect Powell.

Tomás didn't care about that. He loved Henry just because. There was no hidden agenda. He didn't want the Powell money or connections. He didn't want Henry to be pretty and quiet, just another trophy to be shown off. He just wanted Henry.

More importantly, now, with the sun rising over his messy backyard and beautiful chicken coop, Henry was ready to just be himself. He felt free in a way he never had before. Was it embarrassing? Yes. He was an adult, damn it. A night of sex shouldn't affect him this much. It was more than that, though.

The difference between sex with Tomás and sex with anyone else was how it made Henry feel afterward. Tomás's love wasn't possessive or shallow. He'd worshiped Henry, his every touch full of reverence. Henry finally felt comfortable in his own skin. He was where he wanted to be, with who he wanted.

"Everything's gonna be alright," he sang softly. "It's gonna be okay."

He wiped at the tears running down his cheeks, flushing when he noticed Juan watching him from where he leaned against the house. The large alpha was a bit odd. His short mohawk was dyed a deep green and he wore his work clothes – jeans, boots, flannel shirt and a t-shirt with a sasquatch on it.

"Good morning," he said, smiling past his tears. "Tomás is still sleeping inside."

Juan gave him a soft look and sat next to him. "You like Dolly, huh?"

"I've never heard her before." Henry laughed, embarrassed as more tears fell. "Damn it, my eyes won't stop leaking."

"She does that to us all sometimes." Juan leaned over and bumped his shoulder against Henry's. "I like this song a lot. There's nothing more beautiful than a bit of hope after a long fight."

Henry nodded, trying to stifle a sob. "I'm so tired of

pretending to be someone I'm not. Of worrying that I'm not enough. I'm fucking beautiful, damn it."

"You're gorgeous." Juan nodded. "Tomás sees it. We all do."

Henry sobbed harder. "God, the way he makes me feel. He loves me." He gestured to himself. "Me. Hell, when I'm with him, I love me too."

"You deserve that love."

"My last relationship was," Henry struggled to breathe for a moment, "really, really bad. It ended right before I came to Hobson Hills for the first time. He made me feel so bad about myself. I'd never had a lot of self-confidence anyway, but he convinced me I was garbage. Nothing I did was ever right because I was stupid and naïve. No one loved me because I was a disgusting lump of nothingness. The only redeeming quality I had was my money."

"That fucking piece of shit." Juan wrapped an arm around him. "You know that's not true. Right?"

Henry nodded. "I do now, but not at first. I was convinced he was right. He… Keaton," he scowled as he said the name. "He shared me with his friends, and I let him because I thought that was all I was good for." He shivered, tears falling faster. "I've never told anyone this."

"Your story is safe with me, hermanito."

"When I wanted to leave him, Keaton threatened to send pictures of me with them to everyone we knew, including my papa. I stayed like the fool he made me into. No one knew. No one could see what he was doing to me. Everyone thought he was this great guy. If he hadn't dumped me, I don't know what I would have done."

"What would say to your younger self if you could?"

"I would tell him that he's better than a hundred Keatons, and that no one should ever make him feel that way about himself. I'm a good person and I deserve respect."

"You do deserve respect." Juan nodded. "I spent my childhood watching my alpha dad treat my omega dad like a servant. He expected him to cook and clean and look good. That was it. Papa didn't deserve that, but it's how he was raised. It took a long time for him to decide to live for himself. It's a hard thing to do, hermanito. You are braver than you think."

"Thank you," Henry whispered. "I can't believe I dumped all this on you."

"Blame Dolly. She does this to all of us." Juan pressed repeat on his MP3 player. "Come on. It's time to celebrate yourself." He pulled Henry to his feet. "Dance with me."

Henry laughed and sobbed both as he spun around, singing the song along with Juan and Dolly. His body felt weightless, as if he was ready to float away into the sunrise. He couldn't believe he'd told Juan all that stuff about Keaton.

Journey and Mitzy barked, dancing around them excitedly.

"What's going on here?" Tomás leaned against the door, looking sleepy, and smiled as he watched them. Henry enjoyed his stare, feeling the love and joy of it soak into him.

"Oh no." Carter came to stand next to Tomás, shaking his head. "Dolly Parton got another one, didn't she?"

"Juan's going to drag my omega off to his Dolly Parton cult meeting." Tomás sighed, eyes dancing with amusement. "I'm just going to have to accept it."

Juan spun him again. "You'll love our club, Henry. We're Dolly's Diamonds and Dragons. The best club in town. We meet every Tuesday and Thursday at the library."

"I'll be there." Henry closed his eyes, getting dizzy. He let the music fill him, enjoying the moment of pure joy.

"Where have you been?" Audrey greeted him at the door when he got home. His sister looked as perfect as always in her Gucci slip-on heels and black silk jumpsuit.

"You're here?" Henry wrapped his arms around her and settled his head on her shoulder. He was so tired, his emotions wrung dry. Her familiar scent, Baccarat Rouge 540, soothed him. "I love you."

Teague and Sam watched them from the couch, surprised, puppies in their lap waiting to be fed.

"Good night?" Sam asked, smirking.

"The best."

"Where were you?" Audrey grabbed his shoulders and pushed him back. "What's wrong with you. Did you take something? You look high."

"High on Dolly Parton." Henry sat next to Sam and took one of the puppies. "Did you know there's a fan club for her in town?"

"Please tell me you didn't join Dolly's Diamonds and Dragons." Sam groaned. "I guess it's better than Ernie's Bigfoot search group, but only by a little."

"We meet every Tuesday and Thursday." Henry watched the puppy drink from the bottle.

"What is going on here?" Audrey pushed him over, squeezing herself onto the couch next to him. "And where's Journey? You're never without that dog."

"He's playing with his friend Mitzy today." He leaned his head on Audrey's shoulder. "I'm really happy you're here."

"High on Dolly Parton." She shook her head. "What has this town done to you, baby bumblebee?"

Sam snorted. "Be careful, Audrey. It'll get you next."

She gave the three men a disdainful look and stood. "I'm going to your house. I brought some samples I want to show Carter."

"Fine, but don't touch my floor. It's perfect as it is."

She rolled her eyes. "Okay, okay." She strode to the door, then turned around. "Oh, I almost forgot. Papa says you have to come to his charity ball in two weeks. Everyone's going to be there, so he wants all of us present." She smiled sweetly at Teague. "Including the newest addition to the family."

"Say what?" Teague looked horrified.

"You're family now, and the Powell family has responsibilities." Audrey sniffed. "I'll take care of your tuxes. I assume Sam is your plus one?"

"Do I have to go?" Teague asked.

Sam patted his leg. "Sorry, love. Timothy is offering an olive branch by inviting you. We should go."

"Two tuxes then." Audrey nodded and opened the door. "Three if you bring Casey and you really should. Papa is a pushover for babies. Bye-bye."

The room was quiet for a while after she left as they focused on feeding puppies.

"I don't want to go," Teague mumbled, breaking the silence.

"I don't either," Henry admitted, hands shaking as he cupped the puppy close to his face. He hadn't been to a party in New York since Keaton had dumped him. His family was close to Keaton's so the asshole would probably be there. So would all of his so-called the friends. The people who had believed Keaton's lies. "I really don't want to go."

"We'll be there with you," Sam said and squeezed his knee.

Henry couldn't help but smile. He had never told Sam about any of the issues he'd had in New York, but his friend supported him, no matter what. He never pushed or asked questions. He just patiently loved him.

"Well, I haven't seen Papa in months, so I really should go."

Sam set his puppy back into its padded laundry basket bed. "So, how was last night?"

Henry sighed happily. "I'm in love."

"That's so sweet." Sam hugged him.

"Hope Tomás is ready to meet Audrey," Teague said, scowling. "Why do I have to go to a stupid ball. I'm not Cinderella."

Henry ignored his grumbling as the situation really set in. "Shit, Audrey is going to the house where Tomás is."

"She doesn't know about him."

"It doesn't matter. She'll be Audrey all over everything. What if he doesn't like her? Sometimes it's hard to see her good qualities."

"Maybe you should go back." Teague gave him an encouraging look. "We'll cover chores today."

Henry took a deep breath, then shook his head. "No. I need to trust Tomás. Plus, I have responsibilities."

Sam kissed his cheek. "I'm so proud of you. I like you high on Dolly Parton."

"Tomás better keep treating you right," Teague mumbled, scowling again. "He should come to the stupid ball too."

"I'm not doing that to him." Henry shook his head. "Not until I'm absolutely sure Papa won't chase him off."

"What happened to trusting Tomás?" Sam asked, snickering.

# TOMÁS

Tomás let Juan choose the music for the day. He owed him bigtime for whatever he had done with Henry that morning. Tomás had never seen his omega look as free and happy as he had while dancing to one of Juan's favorite songs.

Juan and Carter focused on installing the new counters in the kitchen while Tomás worked on sanding the floors one final time. He'd already completed Columbo's corner, so he put the table and pillows back so Journey and Mitzy had somewhere to sit. The two dogs curled together in the sun, enjoying a late morning nap.

"This looks so much better," a woman said, walking through the front door. She was tall, blonde, and expensive with an air about her that reminded him a bit of Henry.

"You must be Audrey," he said, turning the sander off.

She eyed him for a moment, then stepped forward and held her hand out. "Audrey Powell."

"Tomás Wilson. Over there is Carter and Juan."

"Hi, Ms. Powell." Carter waved then quickly acted busy. "Tomás can answer any questions you have."

She gave his boss a wry look. "I feel so welcomed. Anyway, I brought some samples, Tomás, but my little bumblebee refuses to let me do anything to the floor." She looked the floor over. "I can see why. This is beautiful already."

Tomás smiled, heart beating faster as he remembered how happy Henry was the night before. "Henry loves the floors."

Audrey's eyes narrowed on him. "Hmm, I see. Well, tell me what you think of these wallpaper samples." She pulled a few swatches from the fancy bag she carried.

He looked them over carefully, holding each up to a bare, sheetrock wall. "Okay, so I think he'd like one of these two best, but you really should check with him. This is for an accent wall, right?"

He handed the two designs that reminded him of Henry to her. One was a dark green, textured wallpaper with an abstract design and the other was cream with a simple floral design.

"I see." She studied him for a moment, tapping her chin. "I like you, Tomás. How do you feel about Dolly Parton?"

"I prefer Neil Young."

She smiled at Journey and Mitzy. "Small dogs?"

"Love 'em."

"Cantankerous parrots that swear?"

"They are my absolute favorite."

Audrey grinned. "Light blue dress shirts? My little brother came home this morning wearing one exactly your size."

"His had an accident." Tomás shrugged. "I'm a gentleman, so I gave him mine."

"High on Dolly Parton, my ass. I'll need your measurements." She spun around and went to another wall, holding up one of her swatches. "Henry has a charity ball to attend in two weeks, and I have the feeling he'll want you there. If you can't make it, we have some family friends to step in. Maybe Alistair or Keaton Web."

"Fuck Keaton," Juan yelled, stomping toward them. "That asshole needs my foot up his ass. You can't let him near Henry."

Audrey raised a brow. "I didn't know you were acquainted with the Webs."

Juan patted Tomás's back. Hard. "Tomás will go with Henry. Fit him up nice and all that shit." He glared at Tomás. "You beat the shit out of that Keaton guy if he comes near our Henry. Got it?"

"I feel like there is something you need to tell me about Keaton Web." Audrey gave Juan a pointed look. "Come on now. Tell me."

Juan shook his head. "Just keep him away from Henry."

Tomás and Audrey watched Juan go back to work. "Keaton Web, huh?" he asked.

"My baby bumblebee's ex-boyfriend." Audrey looked him over again. "Get me your measurements by Friday."

"Yes, ma'am."

"Good. Now, tell me about that coffee table in the corner. Where did it come from?"

"My brother made it."

"Does he make other furniture too?"

"Yeah. He can make anything out of wood."

She ran a hand over the old fireplace mantel. The carving was well-done, but had faded over the years. "Henry really loves this place, doesn't he?"

Tomás nodded. "He's happy here."

She gave him a hard look. "You better keep him happy. I want to see him smile every day like he did this morning."

"I'll do my best, ma'am."

She huffed and patted his cheek. "My God, you are so

adorable. Daddy is going to love you. Papa? I'm not sure. He's harder to read."

After that, Audrey buzzed around the place, looking at her swatches and making notes. Carter and Juan tried to keep out of her way, but Tomás chatted with her anytime he had a free moment. He liked Henry's sister. She had a confidence that reminded him of Tali or Hannah.

By lunch time, the new counters and countertops were installed, the floor and stairs sanded, and the HVAC people were installing the new unit.

Audrey sat with the dogs, giving them pets and love.

Two vehicles pulled in one right after the other. Henry got out of the truck and Tomás's papa got out of the car.

"What's happening?" He pressed his face to the window.

Juan chuckled as he watched from beside Tomás. "Your papa brought us lunch. How nice."

"What a coincidence that it happens to be right when Henry was planning on stopping by." Carter shrugged. "Who would have guessed?"

"You texted Papa, didn't you?"

Carter looked offended. "I wouldn't do that. I texted my husband and told him when Henry would be here. *He* texted your papa."

"Nice, he brought fried chicken." Juan sighed happily. "I love your papa."

"Fried food isn't good for you." Audrey came to stand on Tomás's other side. "It's the natural enemy of your arteries."

"They're frenemies," Juan corrected her. "You worry too much. After a piece of Bennett Wilson's chicken, you'll understand."

"He brought Nate too." Tomás pouted as he watched his youngest brother take Henry's hand. "I want to hold Henry's hand."

Bennett's gaze fell on them and sharpened.

"Shit, we better go help him carry things inside." Tomás winced. "That's his *help with groceries* look."

By the time they got outside, Bennett had loaded Henry and Nate with food containers.

"We brought food, Tomás." Nate grinned at him. He still held Henry's hand.

Tomás reminded himself that his little brother was only five.

"I see that, buddy." Tomás didn't have time to say anymore before his papa handed him a box.

"These are more blankets." Bennett leaned up and kissed his cheek. "I think I'm going to like him, son."

"I do." Tomás smiled happily and carried the box inside.

"Audrey, please get Sophie from the car. I want to introduce her to Clucky," Henry said, setting the food onto the coffee table. "Hello, sweetie. Did you enjoy your time with Mitzy?"

Journey pawed at the omega's leg. "Woof."

"I'm glad to hear that, baby boy."

"I can't believe you're making me hold a chicken." Audrey carried Sophie away from her body. "Why is she dressed in a tutu?"

"She likes to feel pretty." Henry took Sophie and hugged her close to him, then kissed Tomás softly. "I'll be right back." He rushed out the back door.

"I knew it." Audrey smirked at him. "You're definitely coming to the charity ball."

Tomás ignored her and pulled Nate into a hug. "Are you hanging with Papa today?"

"We're meeting Henry."

"Don't listen to him." Bennett smiled innocently and handed Juan and Carter plates. "I just wanted to bring my son and his friends a yummy lunch."

"Sure," Tomás said, drawing the word out.

"Put me down. I wanna go see Clucky." Nate patted his shoulders.

Tomás sighed and set his little brother back on his feet. "Papa, can I have some chicken?"

Bennett grinned. "Of course, baby. You can tell me all about Henry while I make you a plate."

BY THE END of the day, Tomás was worn out. His papa had stayed and visited with Henry and Audrey for the rest of the afternoon while Tomás and the others worked and Nate played with the chickens and dogs.

He parked in his drive and smiled. Teague's truck was already there and Henry was at the fence, petting Paulo. The dogs sat on the porch, guarding a familiar laundry basket.

"Are we on puppy duty?" he asked, hugging Henry from behind.

"Do you mind?" Henry leaned back and kissed his chin. "They very kindly gave me last night off, so I thought I'd return the favor."

"I don't mind at all."

Paulo whinnied and bumped his nose to Henry's shoulder.

"I'm sorry. Was I not paying enough attention to you." Henry rubbed the horse's forehead. "I should make a pasture for Paulo at my house. That way he doesn't have to be alone when you stay over."

Henry smiled into the omega's hair. He didn't think Henry really understood what it took to move a horse from one house to another. It wasn't as easy as putting the dog into the car.

"Let's go inside. We can eat the dinner I brought and start watching *Columbo*," Henry said, patting Paulo goodbye.

"Sounds good. What did you bring?" Tomás linked his hand with Henry's and led him across the wet yard and back to the porch.

"Stir fry made by Aunt Mia."

"Sweet."

A few moments later, they sat on the couch with the dogs and their dinner. Henry leaned against his side, pulling one of his new blankets up and around them.

"Wow, *Columbo* is *not* appropriate for kids," Henry said, fifteen minutes into the first episode. "Man is strangling his wife in the first show."

"Never said Abuela wanted me to watch the show." Tomás winced. "Now that I think about it, she did fuss at Abuelo a lot when I stayed up with him."

"That makes sense, but I'm invested now." Henry elbowed him. "I need to see how this goes."

"As long as I get to hold you, I'll watch anything."

Henry snuggled closer to him. "Do you ever think about having kids of your own? A baby to stay up and watch kid appropriate shows with in the evening?"

Tomás was quiet for a moment. "Can I tell you a secret?"

Henry nodded.

"I'm not against having a bio kid of my own, but one day, I'd like to foster or adopt kids like my dads do. There are so many out there like Tali and me that need someone. I think maybe we could be that someone."

"We?" Henry turned to stare at Tomás, eyes wide.

Tomás felt a moment of panic. "It's too soon, right? I'm sorry. Forget I said anything."

"Too late." Henry's eyes watered. "It was too late for me the day I met you. I think I'd like to have a house full of pets and kids that needed me. Everyone deserves love. Just like Journey, Columbo, and Sophie. Like me." He cupped Tomás's face in his hands. "Like you."

Tomás leaned over and buried his face against Henry's neck, nibbling his way down to Henry's shoulder. "I love you. Let's build that home full of love together."

"Okay, I'm pausing the show. No way I can concentrate when you say and do things like that."

Tomás chuckled, then licked and nipped Henry's neck while one hand stroked the omega's dick.

Henry moaned and sank back on the couch. "I can't imagine a home without you in it."

Tomás kissed him softly, then pushed the blanket back. "Can I taste you?"

"Fuck, yes." Henry fumbled as he undid his pants and slid them down his legs. "Absolutely. Please and thank you." He quickly pulled his shirt over his head, tossing it behind the couch.

Tomás trailed his lips down Henry's smooth chest, one hand kneading the muscles like a cat. He bit a nipple, then licked it before doing the same to the other one. He took his time pressing kisses to Henry's soft stomach.

When his mouth reached Henry's dick, Tomás hummed in pleasure. His omega had a beautiful body. He sat up and started working Henry's dick, licking his lips when he saw precum drip from the tip.

He leaned down and swallowed the head, sucking gently, while he stroked the rest of Henry's hard length. Steadily, he took more and more of Henry's dick in his mouth, sucking hard as he went.

Henry gently cupped Tomás's head as he panted. Tomás looked up, enjoying the sight of his omega's face, flushed with arousal.

Tomás pressed his own erection against the couch cushion, hips moving in rhythm with his strokes. He worked Henry's dick for a while, then moved onto his balls, sucking first one, then the other into his mouth.

"Yes, yes, yes!" Henry's grip on his head tightened, then he came, spurting cum between them. Henry barely closed his eyes in time.

Henry panted as he grabbed a napkin from the nearby coffee table. He wiped at Tomás's face. "I'm so sorry, love. I lost control."

Tomás grinned. "No apology needed. That was exactly what I wanted.

Two weeks later, Henry stood in front of the Grand Ballroom of The Pierre, Tomás at his side. The opulent room shimmered brightly, decorated to perfection. The polished sheen of wealth lay over everything, making Henry's stomach dip. This was a world he was familiar with. Beautiful perfection on the outside, icy disdain on the inside.

His papa held a huge charity ball every year. Last year, Henry had managed to avoid it, but this year would be different. There was no reason to avoid anything or anyone.

"What do you think?" He squeezed Tomás's hand. His alpha looked around in amazement. Tomás fit the scenery in his new, perfectly tailored tux and slicked back hair.

"Fancy," Tomás said, shrugging. He smiled at Henry. "I like that chandelier. I think I could make one that big."

Henry snickered. "Where would we put it? It wouldn't fit in either of our houses."

"Finally, you're here." Teague gave him a desperate look. "When can we leave?"

Sam sighed and grabbed his husband's arm. "We haven't even met Henry's papa yet. We haven't met anyone. You need to talk to at least ten people before I'll let you leave. We came all this way, so you can at least do that."

The two men looked sharp in their tuxes. Audrey had done a good job picking out their clothes, even if the four of them were dressed the same as every other man in the room. Sometimes Henry wished he had the flexibility in dressing that Audrey did with these events.

"There's Papa." Henry said, already tired. He wanted to take Tomás and go back to their room. They could lock the world away and order room service.

Milton Powell practically glowed. Surrounded by society's wealthiest, he was in his element. The older omega was trim with rich brown hair and steel gray eyes.

His husband of the moment, Rinaldo Agosti, stood beside him, a handsome accessory. Henry's papa had married three times after his divorce with Dennis Powell. However, he had kept the Powell name through it all and wore it like a badge of honor.

"You boys clean up nicely." Audrey gracefully came to a stop in front of them, a glass of champagne in her hand. She wore a black, sequined Balmain gown and her favorite set of diamonds.

It took him a moment to notice that her smile was brittle, tears shimmering in her eyes.

"What's wrong?" Teague asked, frowning.

"I made a huge mistake," she said, voice shaking. "I should have asked Papa what charity he was raising money for this year, but it's always been the same one, so I didn't think anything about it."

"What is Papa doing?" Sterling, Henry's eldest brother, stomped up behind them, scowling. The large alpha looked dapper in a tux and black rimmed glasses. He also looked furious.

"Hi, it's nice to see you after such a long time," Henry said, sighing. "Yes, I'm doing well. Thanks for asking."

Sterling blinked a few times, reminding Henry of a flustered owl. "Oh, hello Henry." He blinked at Teague. "Nice to see you, Teague."

"Aww, I missed your awkwardness, Sterling." Teague grinned. "It's so fun to watch."

"Now, what's this about Papa's charity this year?" Henry asked, already dreading the answer. If Audrey was upset about it, it couldn't be good.

"He chose your sanctuary," Audrey said, sniffling. "I saw his speech while he was getting dressed. He's trying to embarrass Teague. That's why he invited him."

"He's raising money for our sanctuary?" Teague looked confused. "How is that embarrassing?"

"He wants to make you feel small," Henry said, anger filling him. "To feel like you're out of place here and don't belong."

"I already feel like that." Teague shrugged. "What's the big deal? If we raise money, that's good. Right?"

Sam stomped his foot. "Not if it makes you feel bad about yourself."

Henry closed his eyes and thought for a moment. All the Powell family's friends were there, as well as the leaders of New York high society. He could easily imagine Papa's speech, showcasing Teague as his ex-husband's newest stray in need of their help. It wouldn't be about the animals. It would be about making Teague look like a stupid, poor man that they should all feel sorry for.

He was a little surprised that his papa was doing this. Milton took his charities seriously. "Is his speech really that bad?" he asked Audrey.

She nodded. "It's horrible."

A familiar face drew his attention. "Oh, yay! The Webs just arrived."

Keaton and his brother Alistair followed their parents into the ballroom, smiling and shaking hands as they made their way toward Milton's group.

Henry expected to feel something more than disgust and annoyance at the sight of the man he had avoided for almost two years.

Tomás watched him with kind, brown eyes. "Are you alright?"

Henry slowly grinned. "I am. I really am." He clapped his hands. "Okay. Here's what's going to happen. The opening speech is scheduled to begin in thirty minutes. Sterling, you keep Papa off the fucking stage. Teague, will you go upstairs and get Journey for me? Please put his doggy tux on him and bring the pooch pouch and his treats. Sam, please grab the puppies. Instead of our laundry basket, put them in the container the hotel used for the fruit basket in my room. It should be large enough. If not, grab the one from your room too. Audrey, I need a large piece of black velvet, two decorative boxes no higher than two feet, fashion show background music, and control of the A/V system."

"What are you going to do?" Tomás asked.

"I'm going to raise money for our sanctuary." Henry looked at the group around him. "Get moving."

"On it." Audrey spun around and rushed toward the ballroom door.

"Journey, tux, pouch, treats." Teague pulled Sam along with him and hurried away.

Sterling grunted and stalked toward their papa's group.

"Tomás, it's time to smile and woo the money out of everyone's pockets. Are you ready?"

Tomás grinned. "Not at all, but I'll do whatever you tell me to do."

Over the next thirty minutes, Henry greeted every single person he could, introducing them to Tomás and thanking them for coming to support the sanctuary. It was what Milton was supposed to be doing, but instead, his papa was gossiping with his friends.

Tomás was surprisingly popular with the guests. Henry shouldn't have been surprised. He knew how charming the alpha could be. The guests they spoke with probably found it as refreshing as Henry did to have conversations without any hidden snark or empty flattery.

When the music quieted and the spotlight lit the stage, it was Henry that walked to the podium, not his papa. Sterling stood with Milton, his hand on their papa's shoulder.

He met his papa's gaze, suddenly feeling exhausted. They hadn't seen each other in months, but his papa hadn't come to greet him or showed any interest in speaking to him before the ball.

Milton looked more angry than guilty, as if he hadn't planned on doing anything wrong at all.

Henry focused on the crowd filling the room and smiled his biggest, fakest smile. "My wonderful papa, Milton Powell, is known for his love of charity. For the past twenty-three years, he's held an annual charity ball for the groups he admires the most. This year, he was kind enough to give his own family a chance to ask for help." He gave his papa a sweet smile. "Thank you, Papa."

The crowd politely applauded, and Henry looked out over the crowd, making as much eye contact as he could. "And thank you all so much for coming out tonight to support Furever Home Sanctuary in Hobson Hills, Maine. While most of you may never see the work we do, each and every one of you should feel proud in supporting our no-kill animal sanctuary."

Henry beckoned to Teague and his step-brother came and

stood beside him. "Almost two years ago, my brother, Teague, opened a no-kill animal sanctuary with the goal of offering help to any animal in need. He left his successful veterinary clinic in Washington and moved all the way across the country to a tiny town in Maine. With the help of some wonderful donors, a supportive community, and his own hard work, he has been successful."

The crowd applauded, making Henry's papa scowled.

"Recently, I've invested my own time and money into the sanctuary, officially becoming partners with Teague."

His papa's mouth dropped open and Sterling and Audrey looked surprised.

"When I first went to the sanctuary, I was completely unprepared for what I would find. I expected kennels with dogs and cats and maybe a dingy exam room attached to Teague's house." Henry laughed wryly. "What I found was a wide variety of animals living their best lives in cozy, little homes. For example, we have a whole barn just for our goats. They have their own pasture and playground where they get plenty of enrichment. We keep them well fed and play with them every day. Of course, Teague is there to make sure they all stay healthy with his own top-notch exam room and office."

He tapped his phone and a picture of the goat barn appeared on the screen behind him. It wasn't a professional picture by any means, Teague had taken it quickly. Sam and Henry stood surrounded by the smaller goats as they begged for treats. Their panicked looks had several people laughing.

"These are our smaller sized goats. They *really* like their treat time, but their silly humans forgot to grab the treats before coming in to play."

He pulled up another photo of the goats, these dressed up in donated clothing. "Here are our larger goats. Occasionally they have pajama parties, as you can see."

More laughter filled the room.

"While we have many, many goats, we also have other animals." He showed pictures of the chickens, introducing each one and telling them all about the animal's individual needs and personality.

"This is *my* chicken, Sophie, and her companion, Clucky." The picture showed the two hens pecking at their food, side by side. "I adopted Sophie from the sanctuary a few weeks ago. She was almost dead when she first came to us, but Teague saved her." He leaned over and kissed his brother's cheek, surprising the man. "This man worked for hours to save one lone chicken."

"Many of you may be asking yourself, why is one chicken important?" Henry pulled up a picture of himself with Sophie. He held her close and grinned happily. If he could see the joy in his own eyes, then surely everyone in the room could. "Animals bring people so much happiness. When I'm with Sophie, all the troubles of the world disappear." He smiled at the crowd. "I'm sure many of you have a pet of your own that gives you unconditional love. This is what we offer to our animals at Furever Home Sanctuary."

The applause was louder this time.

Henry squeezed Teague's arm and the alpha went and fetched the basket of puppies from Sam. Henry focused the camera of his phone on the puppies, so their image showed on the large screen. "I want to take this chance to introduce you to our newest residents of the sanctuary. These puppies were brought to us as newborns. Their mama had an extra-large litter and couldn't take care of all her babies, so we were tasked with raising these cuties. For the first two weeks, they needed to be fed every two to three hours. Now that they're a few weeks old, we only have to feed them every six to eight hours." He grinned at the crowd, enjoying the *aww* coming from several people. "We had to drive here from

Maine, so we could bring them with us. While volunteers are taking care of our animals while we're here, Teague and I take our responsibilities very seriously."

Henry's papa stared at him, completely shocked.

Henry stood up. "These puppies will be up for adoption in another month." He smiled and fluttered his eyes. "Just saying."

The crowd laughed again, the mood light and positive.

"Now, as a treat for your patience, I'll introduce you to the absolute best dog in the whole world."

Audrey and Tomás spread a black velvet runner on the stage and arranged two, sparkly white boxes. Henry thought he recognized them from the flower arrangements at the door.

Fashion show music played as Teague led Journey onto the stage. Journey looked adorable in his black tux jacket and bowtie.

The crowd cheered, the guests completely enchanted.

"This is my darling Journey. He was abandoned and living on the streets when a friend of Teague's found him. Due to malnutrition and stress, Journey had lost most of the hair on his body. As you can see, after a year of love and proper care, he has regrown most of his coat."

Henry picked Journey up and looked out over the crowd, stopping on his papa's face. "When an animal comes to us, they are not in the position to be adopted. They have health or behavioral issues that need to be addressed. If they were brought anywhere else, they would be put down with no chance at finding a home. This is because most people only see what is at the surface. They want a pretty dog to show off or a cat to play with only when they feel like it. The animals at our sanctuary don't fit into that perfect picture."

He smiled at his papa, a real smile this time. "We know better, though. Right? Pets give much more than what they receive. They aren't perfect. They may shed or make a mess. Maybe they aren't pretty or fluffy. Maybe they're a bit anti-social. That doesn't mean they don't deserve love."

The crowd applauded again.

Henry took Journey to the velvet run. "Journey had a rough beginning, but now, he's a smart boy who loves me, which makes me one lucky human."

He led Journey through their routine of tricks – running, jumping, and playing dead. Journey perched on top of one of the boxes. "Shake, baby boy," Henry said, laughing happily when Journey held up his paw. "Speak."

"Woof."

Henry hugged Journey as the crowd cheered again. "Without our sanctuary, Journey wouldn't be here with me. Neither would my chicken Sophie or my foul-mouthed parrot, Columbo. Furever Home Sanctuary is doing good work and can use all the help we can get." He smiled one last time. "Again, thank you so much for being here and for your donations. Enjoy the food, company, and music that my papa prepared for you."

The crowd clapped enthusiastically as he left the stage with Journey. Teague grabbed the puppy basket.

As soon as they reached the bottom of the stairs, they were surrounded by people who wanted to see the puppies and Journey. They shared stories of their pets with Teague and Henry and asked about the sanctuary.

"This year, we're planning on adding another goat barn specifically for dairy goats," Henry said. "We have about six at the moment that are lactating, but we don't have room to process their milk. I'd like to make goatmilk soap and sell it in town to bring in some a bit of money for the sanctuary."

"You would?" Teague asked, brows raised.

Henry flushed. "Yes, I would. We already sell chicken and duck eggs in town, but the more we can do, the better."

"There," Mrs. Riverty said, tapping her phone. Her daughter, Rosalie, hung over her shoulder. "I've donated on your website. When you get that goatmilk soap ready, send me some."

"Me too, Henny." Rosalie hugged him. "It's so good to see you."

The Webs approached them next and Audrey stepped forward to greet them. "I'll handle them," she whispered. "Juan seems to think they're not good for your mental health."

Henry leaned into Tomás's side, ignoring the Webs completely. "I really like Juan."

"Hmm," Tomás hugged him. "I'm not sure how to feel about that."

"You must be Tomás." Henry's papa approached, Rinaldo at his side. "Audrey told me about you."

"Papa." Henry nodded, voice cold. It would be a while before he forgave his papa for trying to hurt Teague.

Milton's eyes watered. "Oh, Henry. Don't look at me like that. I'm sorry. I let my pride control me."

"If you're sorry, prove it." Henry rested his head on Tomás's shoulder. "Come visit Hobson Hills next month."

Milton winced. "Isn't your father supposed to be there with that," he looked at Teague, "wonderful new husband of his?"

"Yes." Henry shrugged. "If you're sorry, come for the visit. You haven't even met Teague or his dad. You haven't seen my home either. Plus, it's going to be my birthday. Did you forget like usual?"

Milton sighed. "I'll be there, son."

SEVERAL HOURS LATER, Henry and Tomás lay in bed, Journey

cuddled between them. Henry was exhausted. The emotional rollercoaster of the day was finally taking its toll.

"I can't wait to get home," he said, turning to look at Tomás.

Tomás smiled at him. "You were really good today. You know that, right? I could tell everyone was surprised."

"I'm not usually the family spokesperson." Henry sighed. "It felt good to talk about the sanctuary. I think if it had been any other subject, I would have choked."

"I'm proud of you." Tomás kissed him softly. "I think your papa really is sorry."

"I hope so." Henry frowned. "I don't usually stand up to him, but Teague didn't deserve to be treated like that."

"Always protecting everyone around you." Tomás kissed him again. "I love you."

"I love you too." Henry closed his eyes with a smile, feeling sleep pulling at him. "Today was a good day."

"It really was," Tomás agreed and pulled him closer. "Surprisingly, it really was."

A month later, Neil Young's "Heart of Gold" played as Tomás watched his omega plant flowers in front of *their* home with the help of Nate and his cousin Janelle. Two puppies tried to help them by digging into the dirt and running across the plants they'd just planted.

"Georgie, Lavendar, stop it," Henry said, grabbing the puppies. They weren't quite two-months old, but the two trouble makers held their humans' hearts.

"Dig here, Georgie," Nate ordered, pointing at the ground. The puppy ignored him and started chasing its tail.

Journey and Mitzy avoided the mess and sat on their pillow on the new front porch. The two small dogs enjoyed their new siblings in small doses.

"Quit staring at your omega and get back to work." Tali smacked his shoulder.

Tomás grinned and picked her up in a bearhug, enjoying her annoyed squawks. "Have I told you lately how happy I am?"

"Only every other minute." Tali rolled her eyes and handed him a pot of columbine. Her expression softened as she watched him kneel to dig the hole. "Do you remember when we were at old Ms. Lily's place and you told me that families were overrated?"

"I was so wrong." Tomás shook his head. "So, so wrong."

"You and Henny make a good family." Tali knelt next to him. "You have so many pet-babies, and when you're ready, you're going to be a good dad to human babies too."

"You think so? Sometimes it feels like everything's moving too fast, but then when I'm alone with Henry, it feels like I've known him all my life." Tomás leaned back on his haunches. "Just remember that you can't move in with Tommy when he graduates next year. You're too young. I don't care if it's a Wilson tradition to fall in love quickly. My little sister needs to take her time."

"Tommy and I will move at our own pace." Tali shook her head, looking amused. "Watching the two of you is like watching Dad and Papa. You fit together. I mean, he has better taste then you in almost every way, but somehow it works."

Tomás snorted. "I can't believe you didn't like the furniture in my house."

"My house now." Tali smirked.

"Only after you graduate next week."

Tali had finally talked the dads into accepting that she didn't want to leave Hobson Hills. She planned on moving into Tomás's house since he was living with Henry. She'd take online classes and work on their dad's ranch like she had always wanted.

His other siblings were around somewhere. Hannah and Drew were home from college and volunteering at the sanctuary. Harper and his husband were inside the farmhouse, fixing up the fireplace mantel while Terry was upstairs, painting one of the spare bedrooms. The only one missing was Shawn. Tomás's older brother was in town, working on the old truck they were fixing up for Henry's birthday present.

Tomás made himself focus and worked faster. They were having a birthday dinner for Henry that night. Tomás's family would be there, but so would Henry's. It would be the first time they all met and the first time Milton and Dennis had been in the same room since their divorce. *I hope it doesn't turn into a Koreon soap opera*, he thought, wincing.

The house wasn't finished, not by a long shot, but it was ready enough for company. The outside was still a mess, but the porch was sturdy and the inside looked nice.

Gravel crunched as his dads' car pulled into the drive. Bennett was out of the car before it stopped moving.

"Henry," he called, practically skipping to Tomás's omega. "Happy birthday!"

Henry hugged Bennett tightly. "Hey, Papa Two. Thank you for coming."

Bennett looked at his kids. "You see that? Henry appreciates it when I come by and visit."

Tali groaned. "He doesn't live with you, Papa."

Bennett laughed and pulled Tali into a hug. "I'm going to visit you every single day, peanut."

Tali tried to look annoyed, but Tomás could see the appreciation behind it.

"We brought carrots for Paulo and Apple." Marco, Tomás's alpha dad, held up a bag of veggies.

"Apple," Nate stood, jumping up and down. "I'll feed her."

Tomás's parents had given Henry his birthday present last week. It was a family tradition to go on horse rides together every few months. Apple was Henry's horse. She was a very gentle, gray appaloosa and got along well with his horse, Paulo. They now lived in the small barn and pasture behind the farmhouse, alongside a few of the sanctuary's goats and a miniature donkey.

There were plans to expand the sanctuary onto Henry's property, but it would take a little time. The money was there, though. The charity ball had brought them a lot of new donors.

"Come on Nate, let's feed the horses," Marco said, hugging Tomás and Tali as he passed by. "If I don't do something, your papa will put me to work in the kitchen."

Bennett made a face. "Yeah, yeah. Run away."

Marco grinned and picked up Nate, slinging the giggling boy over his shoulder before striding away.

"Tomás, you'll help me, won't you?" Bennett was the master of the *puppy eyes*. He'd taught it to every one of his children.

"Of course, Papa." He handed a plant to Tali. "Have fun."

She made a face, then grabbed a puppy. "Lavendar, you'll help me dig, right?" She tried her own puppy eyes on the puppy. Lavendar was immune.

Tomás kissed Henry, then followed his papa inside. The house's interior was much improved from a month ago. The kitchen was finished with marble counter tops and sturdy, pine cabinets. A handmade dining table stood out near the kitchen. Harper had taken his time with it, decorating the legs and building matching chairs.

He had also helped Tomás make the wood and crystal chandelier hanging over the living room area. It was a mixture of carved branches and teardrop crystals. The rest of the living room furniture was a mix of wood and brightly colored upholstery. Thanks to Janelle, plants sat on every available surface. Dark green textured wallpaper covered the wall around the fireplace, setting off the beautiful mantel.

Harper waved at him from where he stood next to the mantel, carefully refinishing the old carving. His husband, Grey was already in the kitchen.

"Fuck off," Columbo said from his cage in the corner of the living room.

"Hello to you too, Columbo." The bird had a new ramp to his cage and several low perches. His area was fenced off so the puppies couldn't get to him. They were not nearly as well behaved as Journey and Mitzy, and until they were, Henry and Tomás didn't want to chance the puppies hurting the old parrot.

"Fuck off."

"Woof." Journey trotted inside, Mitzy right behind him.

"Woof," Mitzy added.

"Fuck off."

"Woof."

"Woof."

"Dear lord, that bird." Bennett chuckled. "I love him."

*I love him too*, Tomás thought, listening as his papa began to give him directions. He loved this home full of animals and love. It was his omega's home.

HENRY WAS STILL ELBOW deep in dirt and plants when his papa arrived.

Janelle whistled. "That's a nice car."

Henry sighed. "Papa will only travel in a Rolls Royce." He handed Georgie to Janelle and picked up Lavendar. "I prefer the truck Shawn is fixing up for me."

"You could afford any vehicle you want."

"It wouldn't be the same." He smiled, thinking of the old Chevy Tomás had gotten him. "I'll be right back."

"No worries." Janelle patted his back. Tomás's cousin had become a good friend to Henry. She kind of reminded him of Clucky – super chill and loving.

He reluctantly walked toward the car. The rest of his

family would arrive later that day. He was surprised his papa had come early and not late.

Rinaldo got out of the car first. "Happy birthday, Henry," the man said with a smile. Rinaldo was a nice guy. He'd been Milton's personal trainer for almost as long as Henry had been alive. It had surprised them all when he'd married Henry's papa. There had been no hint of romance between the two men before. At least not that Henry, Audrey, and Sterling could tell.

"Thanks," Henry said, smiling awkwardly.

Rinaldo helped Milton from the car.

His papa stared at him for a long moment. "Henry."

"Papa."

"Your house needs a lot of work."

Henry nodded. "Yes, it does."

"Is that one of those puppies you brought to my charity ball?"

Henry held Lavendar up. "Yep. This is Lavendar. Tomás and I adopted her and Georgie over there."

"Have the other puppies found homes?"

"All but one." Bennett and Marco had taken two and the rest had been adopted out to other Wilsons.

Milton took a deep breath. "Rinaldo and I would like to adopt one if it's possible."

"Huh?" Henry tilted his head, studying his papa. "Who are you and what did you do with my papa?"

Rinaldo chuckled. "Right? He surprised me too."

"Rinaldo likes dogs." Milton pursed his lips. "I also would like a pet."

"Papa, are you serious? A pet is a lot of responsibility."

"I raised three children," Milton snapped. "I'm certain I can take care of a puppy."

"I'll talk to Teague." Henry eyed his papa. "Are you sure you're not an alien?"

Rinaldo laughed. "On that note, I'm going to help this stranger plant some flowers. You two should talk."

Henry handed Lavendar to Milton, smiling as his papa struggled to hold the wiggling puppy. "Follow me."

He led him around the house and down the hill to Sophie and Clucky's coop. The two hens were in the run at the moment, chasing bugs and nibbling at the grass. Tomás had placed a bench nearby so Henry had somewhere to sit as he visited his chickens.

Henry sat down and Milton sat next to him, Lavendar on his lap.

"Why does Rinaldo think we need to talk?" Henry asked.

Milton played with Lavendar's ears. "I'm really sorry about the charity ball. I didn't realize how involved you were in the sanctuary, but even if you weren't, it wasn't a kind thing to do to Teague."

"No, it wasn't." Henry refrained from telling his papa how much of a help it had ended up being. He didn't get the credit for Henry and Teague's accomplishment.

"I'm working on myself," Milton said, reluctantly. "I've come to understand that holding in emotion, be it anger or happiness, is not the best choice."

Henry sat in silence, shocked at his papa's words.

"I'm still upset and bitter about my divorce from your father and that comes out in the worst of ways." Milton shivered. "Ugg, my therapist would be proud of me for saying that, but it *is* true. I love you and Audrey and Sterling. I will try my best to be there for you without letting my anger get in the way."

"Thank you, Papa." Henry wrapped his arms around Milton. "Thank you for apologizing. You know you need to actually apologize to Teague, right?"

"One step at a time." Milton awkwardly patted Henry's back.

"What made you so introspective?" Henry asked, letting go of the other omega.

"Rinaldo." Milton's cheeks flushed red. "Your grandparents would have been so upset with me for marrying him. He's not at all the type of man they would approve of. I resisted my attraction to him for years because of that. When I think of what I could have had with him if I wasn't so worried about how it would look to others, I want to kick myself. Once I realized that, it wasn't hard to see how I've hurt you children over the years."

He gave Henry a fond look. "Oh, I was so proud of you at the ball, Henry. You shine so brightly when you talk about all the animals. I've never seen you like that."

"I *am* rather amazing." Henry grinned. "Have you heard Dolly Parton's song, 'Light of a Clear Blue Morning?' It'll change your life."

"You'll have to explain that to me." Milton laughed.

"Gladly." He wrapped his arm around his papa. "I want you to get to know Tomás too. He's my Rinaldo."

"Then he must be lovely."

"He's my home," Henry said, turning to look at his house. He could see Tomás and Bennett in the kitchen, working on his birthday dinner. "That house right there is a home because Tomás Wilson is inside it. My home."

AUTHOR'S NOTE

Thank you for revisiting Hobson Hills! You may have noticed that this was not Cain's book. I'm sorry, but Henry and Tomás got bossy and made me write their story first. Cain's story will come soon.

ALSO BY C.W. GRAY

***Writing as C.W. Gray***

- **Charybdis Station Chronicles** – *science fiction/fantasy, mpreg*

The Blue Solace Series – series complete

Charybdis Station

Crellic Revival

- The Hobson Hills Omegas – *non-shifter, mpreg, omegaverse*
- Holiday Omegas – holiday stories from the world of The Silver Isles – *paranormal, mpreg, omegaverse*
- The Silver Isles – *paranormal, mermen, mpreg, omegaverse*

***Writing as Chloe Gray***

- A Little Bit of Perfect – *contemporary, non-mpreg, Daddy/Little age play*

If you would like to keep up with releases join C.W. Gray's Reading Nook on Facebook or visit my website at (https://www.cwgray-author.com).

www.ingramcontent.com/pod-product-compliance
Lightning Source LLC
Chambersburg PA
CBHW050010040726
47599CB00014B/1313